PRAISE FOR DUNCAN B. BARLOW

Labyrinthine, lyrical, and provocative, *The City, Awake* is part philosophical mystery, part dream-like meditation on what it means to be human, all wrapped up into a beguiling postmodern puzzle. Buttressed by Barlow's luminous prose, *The City, Awake* takes us on an astonishing journey through the darkened bars and hidden alleyways of an expertly-constructed, claustrophobic cityscape where hitmen are sometimes helpless, where femme fatales are seldom what they seem, and where grit and the angelic mingle on every page—a gorgeous surprise.
— McCormick Templeman

In Barlow's Cincinnati-gone-strange, a germ-obsessed electrified man finds himself at the mercy of a mutant cat man, an odd doctor, misguided policemen, and (perhaps worst of all) the terrors of dating. Unrelentingly bizarre and mysterious, unsettling in all the right ways, *Super Cell Anemia* is a strange and powerful debut.
—Brian Evenson

Of Flesh and Fur is an ancient fable that comes from the not too distant future. Its fevered coyotes worry the bones of fathers who don't have sons, of those who are abandoned and abandon in turn. There's only hunger in these pages, fantasies of manliness that make thin feed. Barlow's spare prose spares us nothing. Read or be eaten.
— Joanna Ruocco

Prepare yourself, good reader, for you are about to have the great fortune of meeting Gilles, dreamer of dark and beautiful dreams, spinner of strange syntax, copper biter, spark shooter, cat chaser, tunnel explorer, vigilant neighbor and, most importantly, hero of this knockout novel. Go ahead, try it, see for yourself (the guy, like the book, is high-voltage) — shake his hand…
—Laird Hunt

ACKNOWLEDGMENTS

James Reich and Hannah Levbarg for taking on my books and giving them love. Emily Vidler for helping edit my Spanish in this book. David Gruber and McCormick Templeman for being early readers of this manuscript.

Matt Bell, Tobias Carroll, Brian Evenson, Sarah Gerard, Laird Hunt, Michael Kimball, Brian Kiteley, Alisa Kuzmina, Kyle and Hilary Noltemeyer, Eric Obenauf, Robert Pennington, Courtney Ranum, Selah Saterstrom, Derek White, my wonderful colleagues at the University of South Dakota who support my writing, and the Sputnik in Denver, Colorado where the earliest draft of this novel began. Finally, I'd like to thank those people, seen and unseen, who have supported my writing over the years.

I reference songs by the following artists in this text: Phosphorescent and Here we go Magic.

A DOG BETWEEN US

ALSO BY DUNCAN B. BARLOW

The City, Awake

Of Flesh and Fur

Super Cell Anemia

A DOG BETWEEN US

DUNCAN B BARLOW

STALKING HORSE PRESS
SANTA FE, NEW MEXICO

A DOG BETWEEN US
Copyright © 2019 by duncan b. barlow
ISBN: 978-0-9991152-7-5
Library of Congress Data Available on Request

First paperback edition published by Stalking Horse Press, April 2019

All rights reserved. Except for brief passages quoted for review or academic purposes, no part of this book may be reproduced, stored in a retrieval system, or transmitted by any means without the written permission of the author and publisher. Published in the United States by Stalking Horse Press.

The characters and events in this book are fictitious. Any similarity to real persons, living or dead, is coincidental and not intended by the author.

www.stalkinghorsepress.com

Design by James Reich

Stalking Horse Press
Santa Fe, New Mexico

For my siblings, Valerie and Scout Barlow, who are thankfully more loving and supportive than the characters depicted in this book.

"[W]e need books that affect us like a disaster, that grieve us deeply, like the death of someone we loved more than ourselves, like being banished into forests far from everyone, like a suicide. A book must be the axe for the frozen sea within us."
—Franz Kafka, a letter to Oskar Pollack

I

FALLING

1

The light catches the edge of a looping crease below the eye, filling valley with shadow. A fingertip to skin, a shift as if to flatten. Youth seems present. Upon release, the sag of flesh holds a print but soon the skin creeps back into form. The occasional speck of toothpaste freckles the mirror. Focusing past the aberrations of silvering and substrate, into the hollows of the eye socket, the curve of the lips, width of nose. He is here somewhere. Imprinted into a chromosome or some such thing. I step back, refocus. There.

Something familiar shifting in the periphery.

This is what it is to miss. My eyes, swelling and red with vein. But then the ghost is gone out of me. Attempting to summon it again, I squint. I bite my lip, turn my head. Still, I am alone. No fatherly ghost stalking in the shadows of my face.

I step into the hall where a doe eyed collie meets me, tail swishing. I run two fingers over Zelda's brow and return to my bedroom, where I've secluded myself since the death.

It doesn't feel so much a death as does it a taking.

There were things that weren't meant to happen. I ease back into my pillow, the buckwheat mizzling. Taking. There was upon the hip, a centipede scar, jellied and yellow. I'd wanted to swat the skin clean of it. The playful wink of the light upon it maddening.

Hand in air, I wipe at nothing. I wipe and wipe as the dog wags her head in tow.

In the morning, the starburst of light stabs me. It has been raining for days straight and the sudden clear day strikes me as mocking. As if Seattle wants to remind me why I'd moved there in the first place—to escape the claustrophobia of Louisville. The bags lay in an awkward abutment, the dog having knocked them in the night. I trundle into the bathroom, where once again, for a moment, I see my father staring from the mirror. I think to say, good morning. Before I can speak, it's me without his ghost. I leave the keys in my mailbox, load my bags, and head for the airport.

On the flight, I peck at my keyboard. Eulogy. What words outline a human life? Something small enough for the audience to digest without discomfort, but large enough to capture the essence of the man's life. Airpocketing. The turbulence almost topples my drink. I catch it, but it sprays the screen. Next to me, a mass of a man; snoring, he eases over the armrest. I wipe the screen dry and close the laptop.

Towing bags, I make my way. Tarmac, Terminal, Concourse. Emma greets me. Her hair, gold and long. Bangs cut precisely over the eyes. She tilts her head and the sheared edges fan. Her arms around me, she kisses my check—the blood beneath her lips warm. This is what it feels like to have something to come home to.

How was the flight, she asks, how are you holding up?

Fine, I reply, and, as well as can be expected.

Never state the important things. After my mother's death, I told only one person. With my father's, three. Colds are public record. Deaths, personal and protected until months later when I can speak with critical distance. It's tough. It's life altering. It's death.

Are you hungry?

Yes.

Pizza?

Naturally.

Emma kisses my cheek again. Takes my hand. She attempts to take the bag from my grasp, but I don't permit it. A speaker overhead blasts public addresses. Travelers shuffle and clamor and squeak and groan.

※

Pizzas slide before us. The grease catching sunlight in small puddles. One hundred eyes wink at me. I shut my eyelids to them and the world is scrapes of metal and Motown songs. Emma leans into me.

Are you okay?

Yes.

Your headaches?

No.

Feeling the awkwardness, the way my hands feel small, my skin gray and thin, my voice too high, I redirect. Alone but moving, always.

I'm exhausted. Just. That.

I know. She says.

No, she doesn't. Still, I smile. Lie, Yes, I know you do.

These are the compromises I've learned to make. Two years have passed since I'd confessed harboring a crush on her for some twelve years. After that night, we've hit and missed in a pattern of turns. This will be different. We both understand the precipice on which we stand. Now or never sort of thing. Whether it's now or it's never, I don't know.

I started my research, she begins, I'm excited to dig into it.

Tell me.

She launches into the specifics as I eat. The mapping of language. The separation of signifier and signified. Some words I remember from graduate school but use in another context. A shared vocabulary with different definitions. I understand the concept, but not quite the why or the how. Something with film. Something with emptying signs. Something with finding the essence of all things. She uses terms like a surgeon uses a scalpel. In conversation, I must be careful. She has a way of speaking that leaves me stumbling—when she wants me to. She can leave me stammering in conversations, grasping desperately at word fragments.

Nodding, I sip my drink, the effervescence tickling my throat. I think of theory I've read: Saussure, Deleuze, Barthes, Kristeva. It has been some time since I've thought of them, let alone read them.

I'm glad you're doing something you love, I say.

I'm making Kentucky home again. It feels good.

I nod.

Somewhere in traffic, a car backfires. The shot vibrates inside my ear's labyrinth. Emma mouths a word and stares at the line of cars. She chews at the word. Over and over again until she's swallowed what she needs and can move on. Then, silence. As my food begins to digest, my body goes cold, my mind loosens. Slipping out of the booth, I nod to Emma. She makes for one last sip of her drink (a seemingly precise combination of Coke and Diet Coke) then follows me out.

The sun falls upon us, its heat the weight of a thousand bodies. We climb into her hybrid car; the air conditioning is slow going. So, we sweat along the roads in the Highlands, passing the old churches, the hip boutiques along the strip, and past the school for dyslexic children, my old school, until we arrive at a blue house with a red door. I unload my bags, Emma grabs her purse, and we walk. Cats and dogs rush the storm door. In the back gloom shifts a body. The light births a face. Bonnie smiles and opens the door. She spreads her arms and steps into me.

I'm sorry, Crag, Bonnie says.

Thank you.

If you need anything.

Staying here is more than enough help.

Your bed is still made up from your last visit.

You've both been so kind, I say

Don't mention it.

I step through the cool shadows of the house as the women talk. The animals follow me, unclipped and clicking against the planks of hardwood. I snake through the dining room, the kitchen, up the twisting staircase, and into the attic. An AC unit hums in the window. The smell of it reminds me of the previous weeks. Of my father thinning from MRSA. The hospital. The gowns. The medical masks. Mommy, my father had called out, I want to be with my mommy.

Oh baby, you look like you've seen a ghost.

I'd not heard Emma on the stairs. Turn to find her just behind me.

Just thinking, I say.

Okay, I'll leave you to think.

I'm fine, I say and sit on the daybed. The air conditioning prickles at my skin.

The dark of the room gathers in Emma's eyes. A skeletal Emma. She reaches at a distance and leans toward me until her hips lock between my knees. I say, flesh. It's a strange word to say. Awkward and biblical upon the lip. Emma catches the word in her mouth. Chews it in silence. She mouths it until it's gone. In her head she has already separated it. There are two pieces in her. I know this. There is no further conversation. Her skin is healthy, well cared for. She has nightly routines, knows the value of flesh. Mine is pallid, my eyes deep-set like my father's, not dark but not quite the same color as my other skin. I think that I should take better care of my skin, then loll onto the bed heavy with sleep. A fetal curl and I'm nearly gone. Emma spoons me. Splays her fingers upon my shoulder. I'm somewhere else. She is present and mapping me. The curve of muscle. The pulse of forthcoming dreams. Soon, she too succumbs, and we sleep until the sun dips into the trees.

2

I stared at the concavities of my father's face. The darkness gathered there in puddles. Just beyond, the machines sat beeping and blinking. The veiny tubes in him streaming away. He lay there. His rotund body like bags of water hanging from pipes.

The surgery had been a success. Though I had nothing to worry about, there was a strange energy needling at my gut. It amplified everything. I wanted the world to hush. The air from the vents to stop hissing. Machines to stop noisemaking. The nurse came in and prodded and poked and made notes. What are you writing, I asked. Readings, she replied. What readings, I asked. Blood pressure, oxygen, temperature, medication, things like that, she replied. I have his prescription list, I said. We know what it is, she said. Last time they almost killed him, I said.

Two years before, he'd fallen and broken ribs. The hospital got his medications wrong. His body weakened and an infection ripened inside him.

My father hadn't wanted me to worry, so he told my siblings not to tell me. Days passed where my father didn't answer his phone. When I'd call my sister, she told me he'd been having phone troubles. I was only privy to the truth when he'd beaten the infection and the doctors had transferred him to a physical rehabilitation center. So quickly his muscles had weakened. So duplicitous his body had been in those days.

I'd arrived just in time to help him return to his apartment. I'd installed a bench in his shower—tethering it to the guiding rail with zip ties. I had pulled against it, lay my weight into it, stood upon it. With my help, my father sat on the plastic seat. His belly hung over his genitals. I could smell them from feet away. I could smell the days of sweat collected in crust around him. He held onto the rails. I ran the water to check the temperature. I toggled the water flow to wet him indirectly. At first, he had tried to wash himself, but the angles proved too much. His strength too weak. Still, he'd tried. I told him it was okay. That he had washed me as a child. I lathered a washcloth with soap. I lifted his stomach, which hung like an udder. I ran the sponge down the seam of his body, along those parts I never wished to see, over the perineum, between his buttocks.

He was able to wash his arms, chest, and armpits. I brought him clean towels. He dried his torso while I dried his lower body. When finished, I led him to his bedroom, helped him put on sweatpants and a shirt. I took to my knee and rubbed liniment oil on the purple skin that flaked along the edges of his feet and shins. Then I rubbed ointments on his yellow toenails and cracked heels. I pulled his compression socks over his feet and led him to the couch so he could watch television. He fell asleep. I watched the breath in him rise and fall.

After the last fall, I'd made a spiral-bound book for him. A checklist of all his medications so he could remember what he'd taken each day. He saved them all. Years of his daily pill routine. Lined against his apartment wall. There was no need for him to save them, but he did. He saved everything.

I had flipped the book over when I'd first arrived at the hospital and began taking notes. I learned this from him. To keep notes. I wrote a list of everyone who came in. Everything they did. Times, dates, procedures, medications, treatments, conversations. The pages filled quickly. When he slept, I entered these notes into my laptop in case the book should go missing. In case we needed to sue the hospital. In case.

I have his prescription list, I said again. The nurse said, yes, I know, and then left us. I walked closer to my father. I bent to kiss his forehead. The smell of his body, putrid. I suppressed my gag and kissed him anyway. His skin was slick with oil. I wanted to dampen a cloth and clean him.

An alarm sounded on one of the machines. The nurse came back and placed the breathing tube back into his nostrils. He likes to pull it out, she said. How many things did I miss when I left the room? How many alarms? I took a seat next to my father. I watched his chest. It scarcely moved. Breathe, I thought. Breathe and tell me a joke.

3

We aren't in Louisville. I lie atop her bed listening to a country singer. He sings, forever is a long, long time. Emma is in the bathroom taking out her contacts, taking off her makeup, brushing her teeth, making herself unpresentable. We aren't in Louisville. Her house smells like mold. Its scent is stronger than the new paint on the walls, the new stain on the floors, the candle she's lit to set the mood. The country singer strums his guitar, loose but urgent, as if his fingers might fall off the strings at any moment. Forever, I think, is a long, long time. I recall the first time I met Emma. There was nothing special about it. I was on a joint reading tour with another author. In another world travelling through hers. I slept on her floor. Barely spoke a word to her. Perhaps her apartment was perfectly appointed. Perhaps she was more radiant than any living thing. I cannot remember. Instead I remember the cat. An oval and spotted thing that trotted into my sleeping bag and purred against my side. So many things we do not see in a life. The world burning bright in a vibrant fire but we choose to see only the shadows. The tremble and wave of the things that occupy us at the moment.

She turns off the faucet and walks into the room in shorts and shirt. Who is this again, she asks. I answer and she says, this is the first night I've slept in the new house. I nod and she says, I'm glad it's with you.

There are kisses and such. I lose my thoughts in curves and sweat. I can smell her body. I can smell the moment she is aroused. I can taste it on her skin like garlic turned steel.

We sleep atop the blankets, our bodies sparkling with gems of perspiration. Tell me about your research, I say and she begins to speak, but I hear little. Instead, I wonder how my father must've have felt after making love to my mother for the first time. How he had felt after filling my mother with me. It's a strange thing, I say, forgetting that I'd asked Emma to speak at all.

It is, she says, language is beautiful and strange.

Yes, language.

The country music comes to an end. It might as well not have been on before, but now that it's finished, the room feels smaller. Emma hugs me, coos like I'm a child. Poor, Crag. I liked your father, she says. He was a sweetheart, she whispers. In truth, my father adored Emma. There was little to dislike. She charms the world. Despite feeling removed from my body, the room, the mattress, I *feel* her. She leans into me and I return to my skin. Am I glowing?

Emma falls asleep. Her head growing heavier with dreams. I wiggle from beneath her. Wander into the bathroom where drywall dust coats the pads of my sweaty feet. The fluorescent light trembles true. I look into the mirror. Soon this state will be my home again. Perhaps, Emma my partner. At least something feels right. It seems like no time has passed since I left Kentucky, but it's been thirteen years. My father had hoped I'd return one day. Eventually, I'd made the plans, but it was too late.

Outside a dog barks against the static of crickets. I pull the skin beneath my eye. It puckers. Slowly eases into place. The dark circles are prickled with light dots.

I return to the bedroom and look in on Emma. Thirteen

years, I say, is a long time to carry a crush. She doesn't respond. I ease back into the bed and stare at the ceiling until light cuts across it. When the birds begin singing, I move to the living room couch and watch the neighbors leave for work. Something shifting inside me—to and against. Some ache for normalcy I know I can never find but that I think I never want.

※

The road to Emma's family estate is shaded by oaks and maples. Stone fences, white fences, black fences, metal fences, houses the size of castles seem to rise and set in the hills beyond the trees. Emma tells me stories of the old families. Some of them had sold their land to Arabs. Sometimes on our road trips, she tells me family secrets. They rest inside me like tumors. Inoperable save for expelling them through language, but I'm sworn to keep them inside, precious and sore.

Proprietatem, idioma, proper, Emma says, seemingly to herself, and then she repeats the first half of a word as if she is trying to say prawn over and over again.

I laugh and this snaps her free from the trance. She pushes a radio station on her satellite service and an Elvis song comes on. I look out at the horse farms. It's all I can stand to hear the song. I wait for it to dawn on her and when it doesn't, I say, Mind if I switch the station?

How can you hate Elvis?
You know I hate Elvis.
Even old Elvis?
All Elvis.
But you like Jonny Cash?
They're not the same man.

She changes the channel to something modern but displeasing. I say nothing. I'm thankful. Elvis was my mother's music. She'd put on an eight-track cassette. Dance around the house with me. This was before the alcohol. Before she died drained and withered. Before Elvis died bloated and high. Before the two of them, forever linked in my mind, shifting and lumbering around in the shadows, haunted me with memories.

Emma steers into a drive that has a stone cottage perched on the edge. This, she tells me, is where my parents would like for me to live. I admire its shire roof. How the bottom edges curl under. Several trees huddle around it to shelter it from the unforgiving sun. Emma stops at a security gate and swipes a card. A long chain pulls the rickety metal gate to the right. It's not long before a bricked mansion emerges from the trees. However, it takes quite a bit longer before I see the full expanse of the building. Without knowing, I sigh.

We aren't rich, she says.

Clearly.

This is all passed down through the family. My parents aren't, she pauses, rich.

I know, I lie.

But I don't know. She had attended, after all, a private boarding school in her teens, gone to an exclusive college, owns two condos in Manhattan and several houses in Kentucky. It's not an issue I'll bring up now. Or ever. I think of my father. Of the year he bought me a towel for Christmas. It was generous. Despite the old towel's condition, its absorbent fibers long since shed, I can't bring myself to trash it, so I keep it in my closet, beneath the extra linens.

We drive past a mansion, curving left beyond decommissioned slave quarters, and descend into fields to the west where the rolling hills crest in the distance—horses punctuating the horizon, small and safe. Although I fear horses, their mammoth skulls looming over me in such a menacing way as if they might strike down at any moment, I can recognize their beauty at a safe distance.

Are these blood stock?

Some, Emma says, but some are just ours.

In the center of the undulating hills, I spy a cozy stone cabin. This is where we stop.

What's this, I ask.

It's where my parents live, Emma says, stepping out of the SUV. As she meets me on my side, she continues, my father moved out here first and told my mother she could come if she liked.

Why?

Emma looks at me and grabs my hand. She puts her mouth next to my ear, it's a family secret. You have to swear not to tell anyone. Swear?

Yes.

My mother had an addiction to drugs and alcohol. She got totally out of control. At the time, my dad was always away with the horse business and she was growing increasingly isolated. When he came home from a particularly long trip to Saudi Arabia, my mother had killed our two dogs. She put the heads on the dining room table for him to find.

Jesus, I stop in my tracks. That's horrible.

It is horrible!

There's a pause and Emma begins again, She's not crazy. She suffers from a mood disorder, or something. I don't know, but my dad…God, I love my dad…He couldn't stand to be in the house after that.

He didn't leave her?

No, he loves my mother so much. He moved into the cabin and she's clean and seeing a therapist. She won't talk to me about it. Even if I ask.

Because you're vegan?

You think, she says.

Does this run in the family, I say, smiling.

No. Just the weird dreams I have. She gets them too.

We approach the cabin and the front door opens. Her father waves to us and two large pit bulls leap out to greet Emma. Yips and jumps and flimsy tongues. Emma takes a knee, pets her dog. She coos to her, rubs her belly when the bitch flips to her back. I introduce myself to Emma's father.

Emma speaks very highly of you, her father says.

All lies, I say.

Her father doesn't smile.

We bend over and pet the dogs. I rake my fingers over the tender nipples of Emma's pit bull. I'm surprised by their softness, find myself uncomfortable for having touched them. I think about my year out of graduate school, of writing copy for a new sex toy company just to make ends meet. The *New Skin Technology* a soft but completely alien texture. *Flesh*, I think again and want to say it.

They're big, I say.

Don't embarrass her. She was a breeding dog. I found her on the streets in New York starving, she says, and, then in a parental voice, says, isn't that right, girl?

I didn't mean to hurt your feelings, Chelsea, I say.

Where's mom, Emma asks.

You know her. She's at the main house doing something. Probably rooting through the attic for some old thing, he says with a wink.

Emma stands and hugs him.

I follow them into the cabin and sit while her father rushes to the closed-circuit television to watch the races.

4

It seemed like the machines were always making noises. A nurse always late to push one button or another. It was impossible to sleep. I eased the recliner back. Turned the lights off. Allowing the glow from the hall to seep in. I worried about my father. I worried that he wasn't sleeping. I worried that the metal they inserted in his hip was hurting him. I worried that he would take too much morphine or not enough. I closed my eyes. I wanted to sleep but found trouble sleeping in the best of situations.

I eased the chair back upright. I opened a notebook and began working. I worked on a story of a mother who had lost her child. Of the killer calling her repeatedly and asking about the dead child. I killed that girl in the first paragraph. I found a rhythm and wrote without distraction until a machine began to beep again. My father awoke, disoriented. Buddy, I called him. Hey buddy, it's okay. I'd never before called my father buddy. He reached under the sheets, scratched. Fidgeted. He pulled his hand free looked at the clear veins running into him. Touched them softly with his palm. Rubbed against the tape. Made to speak but was too high. You had surgery, I reminded him. You're on medication. I like, like the way those kittens are blooming from behind your ears, he told me. They're nice, I said. He slipped his hand into his gown, made a troubled face. What is it, buddy, I said. He yanked free the catheter and howled in pain.

I ran to the nurse's station. Where were they when he yelled? Why were they talking at the nurse's station as if people weren't dying in the rooms around them? He's ripped his catheter free, I said. A larger nurse named Cherry led me back to the room. She made small talk with my father. Despite his inebriated state, he found his charm. He flirted. She lifted his shriveled penis. Reinserted the catheter. He moaned in pain. She pulled the covers over him and fastened restraints to his wrists. She whispered sweet dreams to him. Clicked his morphine.

I'm worried he'll take too much, I said. It's designed to cut him off, she told me. I held my father's hand. It fell slack. His jaw seemed to change shape beneath his skin. It elongated, folded over his top lip. I was unaccustomed to seeing my father without his dentures. His unshaven face looked shorter without them. He'd always warned me to take care of my teeth. If I didn't go to the dentist regularly, he'd remind me. He'd offer to give me money from his social security check. I never accepted.

When I was sure that he'd fallen into a medicated slumber, I stepped outside of the room. I hovered in the doorway, in that no man's land between room and non-room. I watched his chest move and listened to the machines. If I left, would something happen for which I hadn't accounted in the journal? I told the nurse I was going to the bathroom, to notify me when I got back if anything transpired. The last room to the left had changed. The same people sat in the chairs watching their mother die, but they now wore bright yellow robes, clear gloves, white masks.

It was going on thirty hours since I'd left the hospital. The nurse had urged me to go to the cafeteria earlier in the day. There was scarcely food I could eat there. Meat dishes simmering in fatty oils. The grease hardening in pockets. The salad bar ended with open faced buckets of ranch or Italian dressing. Someone had placed the Ranch ladle into the Italian by mistake. The dairy ghosted the surface in swirls. I ended up buying a Diet Pepsi and a granola bar.

Some families were in the hallway watching television or sleeping or arguing or staring into the air. No one is ever happy at the ICU. No one ever jokes or smiles or celebrates. I went to the bathroom. I came out and bought a candy bar. I returned to my father's room and sat down. A man walked in and plugged a tube into the wall. The end of the tube hissed and sprayed a fine mist. I asked him what he was doing. He told me he was giving my father a breathing treatment, spraying Albuterol to help with pneumonia. I said that my father didn't have pneumonia. This will help keep him from getting it, he told me.

The chair was cold when I sat back down. I had asked a nurse for another blanket earlier, but she never brought one to me. How could a patient not get pneumonia in such frigid conditions? I wondered. In the glow of the pale hallway light, I could see my father grasping for more covers. I removed mine and took it to him, laid it over him until he stopped reaching. I wanted to crawl into the bed with him. To rub his arms, his legs, his doughy flesh. Bring the warmth back into him.

I thought of the time I awoke in a hospital bed as a child. I had been hit by a car while riding my bike to get junk food. My father, who lived four hours away at the time, drove from Columbus to Louisville in two hours. He had a bag of candy bars and a six-pack of Pepsi. He said he never wanted me riding to the store for candy and Pepsi again. He never left my side. He slept upright in a chair. Bathed in the sink. My mother brought him food. When I'd wet the bed in my sleep, my father helped them change the sheets, wash me, clothe me.

When my father came to for a moment, he was hungry. I was halfway through my candy bar and he said he'd like some. I eased the candy into his mouth. He pressed his jaws together and gnashed a bite free. For some time, he worked that candy, the caramel tripping him up. I should have considered that. I should have been a better son.

5

I watch Emma as she drives. The afternoon sun is warm upon her face and her skin seems to capture the light and phosphoresce. We leave the highway and drive towards the funeral home. With a kiss, Emma drops me off and leaves to find a natural market.

The funeral home smells of flowers and death. When the door closes, I am blinded for a moment but soon find myself in a world of brasses, carpets, and an otherworldly quiet that nearly crawls into my ears. Before I reach the end of the hall, a man greets me.

May I help you?

Slowly forming in the fog of my vision, first as a faceless golem and then as a stalky little man with an ill-fitting blue suit, the funeral home director approaches me. I can't say how long it takes for me to speak, but I'm made aware that it's longer than it needs to be, as a tweak of annoyance bunches in the corners of his eyes; I'm not above admitting that this pleases me although I can't say why. Just as he inhales to speak again, I introduce myself.

He smiles, a warm but practiced response, and puts his hand out. I'm Jimmy, he begins, you spoke with me on the phone. I'm sorry for your loss.

Thank you. Have my siblings arrived?

Not yet. May I get you a drink, soda, tea, or water?

I shake my head. You said soda.

What, he asks.

Soda, I say, where are you from?

Here, he says.

Originally, I say.

Pennsylvania, he capitulates.

Jimmy leads me into a room with two couches, two chairs, and a long coffee table. This, Jimmy informs me, is where they do business because they understand that it's a delicate time for the family; a traditional office is impersonal. I nod and stare at the empty fireplace. Perhaps in the winter they fill it with logs. Fill it with logs and set them aflame to provide that rustic feeling. To comfort the grieving.

The sound of my sister entering the building disturbs my thoughts. She is loud. Cracking jokes to dispel her grief. My brother is silent but the slog of his dragging feet is unmistakable. My siblings nearly pass the room but correct their misstep and enter. Spreading her arms, freckled and loose around the bone, my sister says, here we are. As if there is reason for celebration. As if our father hadn't died a horribly slow death. As if he isn't on a cooling board in the basement waiting to be committed to fire.

We take our seats and the funeral director begins the drawn-out process of listing options, of paper or plastic, wood or brass, of visitations and services, but never of prices. When I ask about prices, Jimmy rattles off numbers, without a change in his soft, sympathetic register. We will have plastic. We will have no visitation. There will be no viewing of our father's hollowed out corpse. There will be a service. There will be a photo. There will only be a photo. From here until evermore, there will only be photos.

Jimmy leaves the room to generate paperwork. My brother asks about our father's Percocet.

I had the retirement home's manager toss Dad's drugs, I say.

Why the fuck did you do that? That's mine. I'm entitled to it.

Dad wanted it that way.

Goddamn it. He always thinks I'm a drug addict.

My sister laughs, her eyes glassy with tears, That's because you are.

Fuck you. You're an addict too.

I look to the fireplace and say, you don't need it. Just drop it.

My brother stands, paces. He thinks for a moment and, shaking a finger in the air like some intellectual, shouts, I got real physical fucking problems. My back is fucking fucked up. I need those fucking pills.

As the funeral director walks back into the room, my brother straightens up, pulls the sweat stained ball cap off his head, and says, we're just talking about my dad's personal effects.

It's as if Jimmy has some kind of authoritative power. Like he's the police. Like it matters that Jimmy knows my brother's addicted to crack or meth or pills or cocaine. I stand and take the agreement from Jimmy. I check it for accuracy. Sign it. I thank Jimmy for his time and, without looking back to my siblings, leave the building.

The sun feels hotter than before. As if the chill of the dead had held me too long. Emma is in the parking lot, leaning against her SUV. She looks like Jackie O. Some sweet thing from fifty years ago that forgot to age. Her smile is all shimmer and lip, her brown polyester skirt hugging her hips with precision. She has that outward calm at a distance. The confidence and poise of American royalty. That classic beauty of symmetry, clean lines, good bones. My family seems composed entirely of recessive genes, bad posture, aches, and insecurity. Looking at Emma, I feel my body limber, my heart does a funny quiver as if trying to trill. Is it excitement or love? I walk to her but stop short when I hear my sister call after me.

No goodbye, she asks.

I turn and wave.

Things go poorly, Emma asks.

Don't ask, I reply.

We get into the car and Emma hands me a sandwich and cold Diet Pepsi. This is kindness. This is what's missing in life. A person who knows me well enough to get things right. To save me from the world.

As I fumble with the sandwich, Emma asks, who is Juliana?

Who is Juliana, I ask.

Yes, Juliana. Who is she, she says.

I look to my hands, then to Emma. A friend in Seattle. She watches the dog sometimes.

Like now?

Like now.

She nods and starts the truck. Why is she saying she misses you, Emma asks.

I instinctively reach for my pocket and then see my phone on the dashboard. My chest tightens. I say, because we're tight.

That's it?

Yes, that's it.

Okay, Emma says and pulls out of the parking lot.

When we arrive at Jim and Bonnie's house, I don't go for the door; instead, I sit on the porch swing. Emma joins me. The chains moan with our sway. Neither of us speaks. Not at first. After a few minutes, I say, I remember watching you on this swing last year. You looked lovely.

I remember that night too. It was fun. Emma looks at me and then away and says, and then you dumped me and lied to me.

I didn't dump you.

What do you call it?

I call it nothing. I thought we were trying it out. Didn't want anything long distance. This is what I say. Her temper flushes her face. This is the ongoing argument. Did I date another woman immediately upon my return or didn't I? I say, no. Emma says, yes. She says, bullshit. She gets upset.

You left out the lying, she said.

There's a dog across the street that's tethered to a tree. His golden fleece wavy along his lean flanks. He takes to barking at us for a while, but tires of it and circles down for a nap.

Whatever the right thing is to say here, I know I'm going to miss it by a mile, I offer.

The fact that you think there's a *right* thing to say, worries me.

I don't mean it that way. I mean that I didn't lie to you, but no matter what I say…I trail off thinking of the times where she saw me texting someone and asked who it was, all those months ago, and I said a friend. Though it was true, I knew there was the distinct possibility that the particular friend in question could have become more if certain circumstances would've arisen, which they did, and we were. Was it a lie? Should I have said that she was a woman that I liked but who only seems interested in me when I was away? That I might have dated her if Emma didn't commit to me? Maybe I had fooled myself into thinking it was nothing. Whatever the case, nothing I say will make this moment pass any easier.

I didn't lie, I say.

Then we argue. She digs in and when I counter she dissects my words, turns them inside out, leaves them bleeding here in the fine angle of sun on the wooden porch. I retreat into myself. Saying less and less until I say nothing at all and only listen to Emma as she processes her thoughts. Eventually, she sees the sorrow in my eyes. Heavily, she perches her head upon my shoulder. It's not an apology. It's a truce and I'm willing to accept it, and though it's hot outside and her touch makes me sweat, I dare not move. This is one of those crystalline moments that may set a rhythm forever. Still, it seems to possess an otherworldly weight.

She begins to talk of her ex, a mad actor with a penchant for drink. He was a pendulum of anger and social grace. Beloved by fans and handled with kid gloves by friends and family alike. He was nearly twice her age. She says that her brother calls him ol' slack because of his lazy eye. This makes me laugh. I repeat the name. Emma laughs. She says eventually she had to out-crazy him, attack him to end it for good. Break it beyond repair. This, she says, is how she handles things. Breaks them until they are irreparable. This won't happen with us, she says. We're best friends. Her head weighs more than the Earth and the Moon and I say, let's go inside.

6

My father asked why my brother was crawling around the ceiling. He stared at the tiles. I said that my brother was checking in on him. That he wanted to make sure my father was well. He furrowed his brow. Cocked his head. He was trying to figure out how my brother was able to do it. I attempted to wake him, clear the fog from his thoughts by asking questions. To needle and prod. To distract him. Soon, my efforts paid off. He responded to my inquiries. How was he feeling? Did he know where he was? When was his birthday? Who was the president?

Sometimes these questions yielded unexpected results. He, for example, once asked what I had done with Crag. He believed that I was an imposter who was holding him prisoner in a warehouse. Where is my fucking son, he asked. This particular bout of paranoia began while I was away—having a long overdue shower and change of clothes. My father's friend had been watching a TV show about a Navy crime investigation unit. Submerged in the murky depths of a medicated slumber, my father was inundated with titillating and complex plots, which somehow meshed themselves with his sense of reality. When I returned to his side that day, he awoke, convinced that he was part of a world of conspiracies, betrayal, murder, and espionage. I'd only been gone a couple hours, but that was long enough for him to believe that I wasn't me but some operative sent to excise high security information from him. What he thought that information was, I had no idea. I knew I had to divert him, so I talked to him about the spring weather, about how good he was looking, about how much of a warrior he was.

My heart seemed to quiver in my chest. Seeing my father so terrified, so convinced he was being held against his will, crushed me. It was only later, years beyond that moment, when the echo of it rang out in an unexpected place, that I understood that he had been a prisoner.

Again, I found myself calling him buddy. The orderly arrived with a cart of food. Hamburger. Pickle. Mashed Potatoes. Diet Pepsi. Yoghurt. My father hadn't eaten in days. He asked for the yoghurt. I opened it. What flavor is it, he asked. Strawberry, I told him. Oh goodie, he said, that's my favorite. With the spoon, I scooped a small bite free and fed it to him. He slicked it around inside his mouth. He popped and slurped and swallowed. He opened his mouth again. I fed him more. We repeated this until he grew thirsty. I held the cup with a bendy straw. He drank. Sloshed the effervescent Diet Pepsi around. He opened his mouth and released a gasp of pleasure. With his weak and trembling hands, he grabbed the burger. He gnashed it between his jaws. It seemed to take a lifetime for him to swallow it. I offered a drink. He drank.

The sun rested on his face. I snapped a photograph. The right side. Shadows deep and sinister. At the time, I took the photos for him so that we could sit together when he was better and I could say things like, I'm glad you made it through. You are one of the lucky ones; seventy percent of all seniors die from post-surgery complications. It's a beautiful photo, someone would say after.

He put down the burger. Fussed with the pieces of paper on the bed table. Fussed with the can. Knocked the can over. I picked it up. What do you want, I asked. Is there more yoghurt, he asked. No, you ate it all, buddy, I said. Why was I calling my father buddy? I went to the nurses' station. I asked if we could get more yoghurt. He likes strawberry, I told them. I turned around and noticed that the family in the room next to us were wearing yellow gowns. They'd not been wearing them when I came in. Perhaps, I thought, that is what happened when the patient got pneumonia. Something to protect the compromised immune system against the germs of the outside world.

By the time I came back into his room, he was asleep. I rolled the table away. I covered it. I tucked him in. I stood there and watched his chest rise and settle. When my mother had died, I saw her chest sink and never again rise. I fell to her side and checked her pulse. It was how I understood death, a sinking chest. Sometimes my father's chest would take forever to rise. When this would happen, I'd hold my breath. I'd look at the computer monitor to see his heartbeat. Even with the pulse moving across the screen, I wouldn't release my own breath until I'd see my father do the same. He was always pulling the breathing tube from his nose. Toss it. Drop it. Leave it on his head like a pair of sunglasses. The monitor would beep. It would beep until someone put the breathing apparatus back in his nostrils. If I didn't do it, a nurse would. The nurses, however, were slow to respond and this didn't sit well with me. It scared me to death.

The nurse eventually came back and told me that they had put yoghurts and my father's preferred cola, Diet Pepsi, in their personal fridge—it's harder to get Pepsi in the south. We really like your dad, she said. He's a charmer. This was true. Women adored him. He was funny and kind and intelligent and strong. I'd forgotten this until I'd seen him at the retirement home with all the older women competing for his attention.

After living in the isolation of the countryside for twenty years, my father finally grew too fragile to live on his own. His blood too unpredictable. His legs too unsteady. Whereas the country home with its broken plumbing, lack of central heat, and broken walls, deterred me from returning home for visits, the retirement home gave me hope. I visited more often. As I watched my father sleep in the hospital bed, a weight fell upon my tongue, a fragment of something I could not speak: I should have come home. When his legs went blue with diabetes, I should have moved home. Rubbed lotion on them. Helped him with his compression socks. I should have been to him what a son should be. Instead, I lived on the coast and loved and lost and wrote. Until the bones of my father's corporality pushed through the canvas of my constructs.

He'd been so good at making me believe he was always strong. Even when he had a walking cane, he looked like he could knock a truck from its wheels. The truth was there in front of me. Hanging from the bone. Fatty, pale, thinning. I stood, walked to the window. Looked over the city as the afternoon sun ran down the buildings. Traffic molted through exits, slow and writhing. The air conditioning kicked on. My skin rose in bumps. I returned to my father's side and made sure his blankets were snug against him. His hands held on to the edge of the sheet. His fingers undulated around it as if it were a bar to hold him down. As if he were in a car about to creak up a hill and soar down into a winding ride. Pricked for blood and medicine, his hands were spotted purple and red.

On the spots where there were still tubes running into him, clear medical tape made his skin look wet and sickly. One it was, the other it was not. I ran my fingertip over the tape, avoiding the sensitive areas around the needle. He'd grown used to needles and pricks. His diabetes required constant sacrifice. To monitor. To regulate. I had watched him monitor it. When he seemed to get dreamy or weak, he'd realize he'd not eaten or that he'd perhaps had too much sugar and his blood was angry. Or whatever he would say. There was always an old tin coffee can filled with used needles and test strips on his table at home.

7

When my heartbeat is up, I transition into a run. The sun, lowly slinking, casts long and thickening shadows, as bugs resurrect to feed. I smack my skin, push my body. Some of the bites begin to itch, to sting. I run through the winding streets, around the middle school, past the Irish bar, through the cemetery, and finally reach my father's retirement home where I slow my pace and look to the dark window that was once my father's. In the shadowy room, all of my father's things are in their right places. His pill bottles arranged in order. His dirty dishes stacked in the sink waiting for their morning scrub. His towel hanging from the rack.

The next morning I will begin the daunting task of clearing the apartment. Make sure the grandfather clock goes to my cousin, the family china (mostly chipped) and other heirlooms (mostly broken) aren't pawned, remaining pain pills tossed. I think of the yoghurts in the fridge, of the bars of white soap in the closet, of the stacks of ice trays in the freezer. All of it soon to be tossed, the work of my father erased.

The night creeps behind this moment where flowers phosphoresce in the crepuscular gloom. I arrange words in sequences. Think of how I'll write about this. One day. I have always written about death. About sadness. Yet, when I'm in the mouth of it, I'm devoid of language. How many days did I sit there in silence, staring at my father?

A lightning bug pulses in the air before me. When I was a boy, we would catch them. Smash them. Harvest their temporary glow. Spread it upon our faces like war paint. I reach for the bug. Cup my hands around it. It crawls on me. There is no panic to get away. The bug is slow. Nearly trusting. This is why they are so easy to kill. It crawls onto the backside of my hand. I lift my arm. The bug spreads its wings. Takes flight.

Childhood is filled with murder. Children put wooly worms in jars with leaves. Smash spiders. Pull legs off daddy long legs. There are kits that encourage this. Parents absent in moral forethought, buy them in chain stores, bring them home. Kids run through the yard capturing alluring insects like wooly worms, butterflies, and lightning bugs. They place them on their dressers and watch as the bugs grow lethargic, as they starve to death, as their legs curl up and the husks of their bodies lay dried. I wonder if this gives us permission. If we are trained to kill first through wonder. The dominion of the larger.

I touch my face, feel the skin. Despite the sweat, It feels temporary and thin. My body is filled with vague aches, explosions of synapses flowering in the dark of my body, and I wonder if this is how it begins, the gradual slide from middle-age to being a septuagenarian whose muscles can no longer support him, his nerve casings loose, his movements ill-timed. I launch back into a run, harder this time, my heart a raging hammer.

By the time I get back, Emma is waiting with her dog. Chelsea runs to me. She lies on her back. I rub her. Talk sweet. Kiss her head.

She really likes you. Emma says, walking over.
I really like her. Don't I, Chelsea?
We go inside, into the attic. I prepare some things for

a shower. I toss my phone onto the bed. It bounces, lands face up. Emma takes out a tablet. Looks through some pages. Checks some stocks. I am searching for a clean pair of underwear when Emma says, why the fuck is your friend putting hearts in her text messages?

I stand up. Flip between two pairs of socks. I know I've looked too long. Answered too little. The light from the table lamp rests on half of her face. Her bangs appear measured. Her eyes forever deep. She works the muscles in her jaws.

We're close, I answer, feeling as if the words are shattering upon the ground as they leave my mouth.

Why don't you hire a professional?

Because I don't know when I'll be back.

She returns her fingers to her tablet. It brightens and blooms into a ghostly glow upon her face. I don't really care, she says, it's just odd.

I sit on the bed, scoop the phone into my hand, look into her eyes. Clearly, you care.

I just think it's bullshit, she says.

What?

Couldn't you find someone else? Someone who doesn't like you?

What makes you think she's so keen on me?

Do your guy friends text you hearts?

Juliana is good with Zelda.

Go shower.

I leave the room. I slink down the steps and into the bathroom. I look at the message: I hope you're okay. Less than three. I run the water and get in. Hot water pounds my back. My muscles seem to loosen. Something works at my mind. A small animal scratching to get out. I'm exhausted. Mind too busy with boxing things. My heart too dead to hurt. An impulse to cry comes. A tremble at the lip. Bulge in the throat.

Yet, nothing happens. I imagine my father as he was before the fall. His humor. His generosity. I try to recall the feeling of his arms around me. How these things, these physical things do not seem to translate into memory. Leaning into the tiles, I slide my head, pushing as hard as I can. Back and forth.

When I return upstairs, Emma has couched her anger. She lies with the dog. Stroking her head. Speaking in words I can't understand. Latin. Greek. Something ancient. I join them. Chelsea butts her forehead against mine. Licks my mouth. I wipe it clear. Laugh. Emma reaches her arm over the dog, onto me. I want it to sink into me. Puncture the skin and rub the surface of my heart. Warm me and make the pulse feel human and not mechanical.

I'm not sure how long we lie there before we fall asleep, but when I awake, it's to a crash of thunder that rattles the house. Chelsea is whining. She has crawled over to me and buried her head in my chest. Worried that the lightning might strike the air conditioner, I wiggle free of the dog, walk across the room, and shut it off. Chelsea follows me. Emma sits up. Her torso nearly perpendicular to bed. She slides her feet onto the floor. As if on wheels, she drifts to the dog and drops to her knees. She pets the coat, rubs the belly, fingers the tender meat between the ears. She looks to be playing a Theremin. Her hands light upon every touch. She speaks. They're not words. Sounds. Sounds that seem like words.

What are you saying? I ask.

Emma doesn't respond. She pets the dog and coos in her secret language.

Emma, what are you doing?

Again, she doesn't answer. I blow air through my nose and return to the bed. There's no time for passive aggressiveness. I need sleep. On my side, I stare into the darkened room. I hear the dog and Emma, but can't see them. A streak of lightning splits the sky and I see their outlines. Specters among the shadows. When the thunder hits, Chelsea rattles her claws, yips. Emma, her back to me, her hair long and pale in the tremors of lightning, seems vacant. As the rain and hail begin to pelt the roof, I return to them and urge Emma to bed.

What the fuck, Emma asks in a way that sounds more declarative than inquisitive.

What are you doing? I reply.

I don't know. Sleep walking?

Get back into bed, I say.

We ride out the storm. A dog between us.

8

Another family began wearing yellow robes and facemasks. I sat across from my father who was beginning to look better. He spoke to me sometimes. He told me his face itched. He asked for Diet Pepsi. He told me he had to piss. He told me he had to shit. The nurses worried that he might not be able to urinate. They worried his kidneys might be the issue. They requested a sonogram. I waited for the technician to come. These things seemed to take forever. I wanted to sleep. I closed my eyes and felt my body grow light. I saw the white lightning of my veins against my lids. I felt the pulse in my sockets. I was drifting until a machine beeped. My father looked around him, his eyes wide. What is that, he asked. What is *that* beeping?

Dad, I said to him, you can't pull your breathing tube out. I walked over and helped him replace it. His ears were red and chaffed from the rubber. I could tell it hurt. I wanted to rub lotion on him. I wanted to put a bandage in-between his flesh and the tubes. The machine stopped beeping. My father folded his hands and rested them on his belly. He sighed and closed his eyes. I told him I loved him. He didn't reply because he was already asleep.

By the time the technician came, I was ravenous, my patience thin. She looked at a clipboard and rolled a machine into the room. She didn't look at me. She didn't speak to me. I prompted her. Forced her out of denying my presence. I asked her to explain the process. This seemed to bother her. Explaining her job. I watched her take down the sheets, lift the gown, expose the gray of my father's flesh.

She coated two wands in gel. Touched buttons. Eased them onto my father's skin. Slipped them around his stomach, sides, under him. Pushed buttons. Looked at the screen. Pushed buttons. He moaned. She stared at the screen. She hemmed. She hawed. I asked her what was wrong. A mass, she said, or a fog. A fog, I asked. A fog, she confirmed. She called a nurse into the room. Asked to have my father rolled to his side. His left, I urged. A nurse once rolled him on his bad right hip. Hurt him. She should have known better.

The nurse called in another. They gently rocked my father. They counted to three. They rolled him onto his side. My father passed gas. It was wet and loud and never seemed to end. The nurses laughed. The technician used the wands. The fog is gone, she told us. I laughed. My father laughed and said, how'd you like that one? One nurse said, not at all. The other complimented him. I liked the second nurse. She was kind. She joked with my father. Allowed him to be cute.

When I was young, my family had to attend a wake. My parents didn't allow us to view the body. They told us to play with the other children in the room where the food and drinks were. They told us not to touch the alcohol. Eventually the family came back, some of them crying. Some laughed and talked about the man in the casket, my grandmother's husband. My father went into the bathroom. He passed gas. It too was loud and long. The room laughed, even those crying. He came out to the laughter, blushed, and asked if we liked it.

It wasn't his kidneys they determined. They took the catheter out. He yelped, said, goddamn. A nurse brought in a plastic jar with an angled top. The friendly nurse pulled the head of my father's penis into her fingers, slipped it into the jar. He sat there for some time dipping between this world and that. We need you to try to relieve yourself, she said. He grunted. He tried. A small amount came out. She gave up and said she'd try again later.

My father fell asleep, his penis still showing. I walked over to cover him. I could smell his stink. Fermented corn or something dying. He'd not been bathed in some time. I held my breath and pulled his gown back into position. Lifted the sheets. I found his lotion. I rubbed it into his purple calloused feet. They were cold. I applied pressure while I rubbed. I bent over them, cupped my hands around one, breathed onto it, rubbed it. Afterwards, I washed my hands and visited the nurses' station. He needs a wash, I said. The nurse who was not nice looked away from her computer and said that she'd come in and clean him in a few minutes. I told her that they shouldn't disturb him. That they should let the old man rest. She rolled her eyes and said, later then.

When I returned to the room, my father warned me that he was going to explode. He had to piss, he said. It happened that a physical therapist arrived. She said that she would help him. Together, she, the nurse, and I helped my father upright and to the side of the bed, so his feet could hang down. He sat there, slumped in pain. His back exposed. He looked so vulnerable. His gray hair disheveled, skin seeming to fall away from him. They wrapped a nylon belt around his back. Eased him forward. He made to stand. Titled forward, almost falling. They corrected his fall. The nurse inserted him into the bottle. People passing by could see it. I pulled the privacy curtain shut. I heard his urine stream, hammering the plastic jar. He moaned, half in pain. The urine was dark and that worried me. I worried his kidneys were compromised. I worried that he was going to die. I worried that he would never walk again. He was so frail.

They eased him back onto the edge of the bed. I helped them by pulling his feet over. The nice nurse came in with a tub and supplies. She told him they were going to take a bath together. My father, exhausted by exercise, said, not tonight, baby, I've got a headache. She laughed and said that someone had complained about the smell. He asked if it was his pain in the ass son. I laughed. I told him it was me. He laughed. I helped the nice nurse clean him. I lifted his belly as she washed his privates. I made fun of his genitals. He laughed, called me a little prick. She worked on other parts and I dried him. I could feel his flaccid penis through the towel. His lopsided testicles. The sagging flesh of his buttocks. He asked if I was enjoying it. I told him that I was not. I told him it was what people do out of love.

The nurse lathered his face. She soaked the blade to warm it. She made to cut his facial hair. Her hands moved about his chin. She nicked him and grew nervous. His beard is very tough, she said. I stepped in. I rubbed his cheek. Felt the coarseness of his hair much like my own. I went to the bathroom with the tub. Emptied it. Ran hot water. I dumped washcloths into the container. Let them soak. When I brought it back, I placed the washcloths on his face, and let them sit to soften his hair. After I removed the rags, I reapplied shaving cream and pulled the blade along his cheek. The hair came away a bit easier. My father slept. I did what I could. Skipping a few of the tougher places. I woke him to shave his neck. When I'd cleared most of the hair, I washed him with a damp cloth. Toweled him off with a dry one. In a hushed tone he said, thank you. Fell to sleep. I kissed his forehead.

9

The apartment is haunted by his smell. A bulge rises in my throat, gummy. I can't seem to swallow. This would be the time, alone with my father's possessions, I could break down and cry. However, I can't bring myself to do it. Almost as if my father is present. The way I showed no fear in the hospital. Everything was going to be fine. See how I smiled? See how I congratulated him on his steps towards healing? Good work, buddy.

On the table, a photograph of the President and his wife framed in metal. Something from the thrift store. Below the photo, a stack of bills, medical receipts, Medicare forms. Old age is nothing but managing paperwork, jumping hoops, and doctor's visits.

Arbitrarily, perhaps, I check a closet. Boxes stacked to my nose. I open one to find a lifetime of tax forms and receipts. The next, a collection of old mugs, many of which I remember from childhood, a few Santa heads, a camel, one of Garfield leaning on a counter—he hates Mondays. We used to drink hot cocoa from the Santa mugs on Christmas eve. Next to the fire, by the tree with its large multi-colored bulbs. Before the unemployment. Before poverty. Another box is filled with my old ribbons, childhood art projects, photos, and such. This is what a father does. Carries lifetimes on his back. The archivist of those achievements and mementos that we children left behind, forgot. I can barely stand to look at it. To recall all the love of my father. How it hangs above me like a guillotine.

I walk into the bathroom. The smell, mold and cheap soap. I flip the switch and look into the mirror. The shadows of my eye sockets. There, where the memory is most haunting. Wide and lazy eyed. I see him. A smile and it's complete. The mouth and nose are most like him when I smile. It's a crooked smile. Slant upon the face. A dip of flesh. Dimple. I tell the ghost of my father that haunts my face that I miss him. The ghost mimics me. A fingertip pressing against the mirror. Unable to penetrate the veil between the living and the dead. More pressure. The glass bends. More pressure. Maybe. How many days had I seen the full moon of my father's face? Thousands of times, but never had I thought, this might be the last time. And now I have nothing but photographs and a thin genetic shadow of him ghosting my face. Can a person drink in a full cup of sight? See it enough so that *that* one vision is enough for the rest of his life? Then I think of standing against the bole of Devil's Tower with my friends. Looking over the vast prairies that surround it, knowing that would be our last adventure together before we took jobs, got married, lost ourselves in drugs and died. I wanted to drink the sky so deeply that I'd never forget it, but now, just like those thousands of times I saw my father, that moment seems faded and dried, my memory parched.

My phone startles me. I finger it out of my pocket. Touch the screen. Answer. Emma tells me about her morning. About her yoga. About her words. About her lab. About things I can't understand. Things that, if I could understand, still wouldn't make sense. Her energy is contagious. Always was and always will be. My heart gives a strange beat. Excitement. I am sweating and can't remember why. Emma asks if she should come in town that evening. If I need space. But I don't understand space anymore. The world has collapsed on me. The air, the boxes, the language. All of it falling on top of me. Inside me. Through me. Endless falling until I am full of the world and the world is pushing out against my skin. Until I'm split through with everyone and everything and there's nothing left. I'm quiet for a long period of time. Emma asks if I'm okay.

I don't know, I say. There is so much, I say.

So much what, she asks.

So much of the world, I say. So much history that wants to be recovered.

It's natural, she says.

I want to ask her who she's lost. I want to ask her about her saddest moment. I want to ask her what her father smells like. Ask her if she could bear smelling him after death. Ask how she'd feel if she watched her mother die. Ask how she would feel if her father died in a room with no loved ones around him? My pulse grows uneven. My breath short. I bite against my lip. I'm on the verge of saying it, of telling her that her words ring hollow, prepared, to tell her to fuck off for a while. I press my heel against the toilet seat, increase the pressure. It resists, then begins to slide, dried piss breaking away from the plastic screws at its base. Then, it snaps free and rattles between the john and the tub. I want kick holes in the floor.

What was that, she says.

I dropped something, I say—the words barely audible.

She says, I love you.

It catches me off guard. Love is something I feel dying all around me. It's boxed and spread across a table. It's sealed in prescription bottles. Resting in the sink. Cooling in the fridge. It's stacked by the bed and hanging on racks. I walk out of the bathroom, stare out the window, see the dogwood blooms swaying in the breeze. I think of forests burning. Love.

I love you too, I say.

They are words that come without preparation. As they leave my mouth, they seem stranger than hers. As if my words have a different center of gravity.

We make plans for the night. Dinner and a walk. Something outside of moving boxes and stuffing bags. When we're done, I return to the room. Begin tossing medical supplies into bags. Move to the paperwork and divide the necessary from the unnecessary. My father saved everything from multiple copies of pharmaceutical warnings, to pharmacy bags, to pill bottles, to postcards and letters. He has forty-year-old contracts from his restaurant consulting business. He has statements from his credit cards, divorce papers, past bills, everything stored in stacks of milk crates. After several hours, time marked by the emptying of drawers, opening of files, filling of bags, that impossible task of deciding what is important and what is purely sentimental, I take the waste to the dumpster.

The sun is hot. I sweat. The school next to the apartments lets students out. They run to cars, to buses, to sidewalks. To journey home. My sister is a teacher there, but doesn't emerge with the kids. She doesn't walk to her car. Doesn't come across the street to help. I look at my phone. I check my work email. I check on the movers who will take my boxed life and place it in a moving truck. I check on Zelda. I consider sitting on my father's favorite bench next to a small maple tree. Where we'd watch the squirrels and wait for my sister to come over after work. My father would tease her and I'd come to her defense.

When I arrive, I find another old man sitting on the bench, his white dog keeping the squirrels at bay. It's an old man my father had tussled with in the dining room over politics many times. Some old conservative who my father said hated the President because he was black more than the fact that he was a Democrat. My father always called me after their heated debates, and though I know my father loved a good argument, something about these fights really seemed to stick with him. I think of my father praising Reagan in the eighties, of his shift to the left in later years. Some kind of pride blossomed in my chest, warm and swirling and I'm tempted to approach the man on the bench. To sit down. Make him uncomfortable enough to leave so that squirrels can come down and play. Instead, I return to lock up the apartment, where the remainder of my father's worldly belongings are unceremoniously unfurled, as if I'd cut along the belly and disemboweled the place. It seems like I've only made things worse. The unsettled nature of the room haunts me, but I know I have to leave. Another hour here will ruin me. Every time I close the door, there seems to be an awful finality to it—a finite countdown before the guillotine blade finally falls.

※

The dirt runs off me in torrents, pools at my feet, and eventually slithers into the drain. How much of my skin leaves me? How much of my father's DNA sloughed and rinsed away, drifting with the millions of others along the creeks and streams, the Ohio River, the Mississippi, the ocean? My heart doesn't seem to beat but I can feel my pulse when I place my fingers upon my wrist. Though I feel divorced from my emotions, I sense the heavy hand of sorrow near me at all times, gripping just tighter in small increments. This is what loss feels like. To pretend everything is normal. Life will never be okay. That part of me is dead now. A part of me will never come back. The world has become less steady. The universe a skin tent poked through with holes. Held aloft by decaying bones. I am moving through it step-by-step; if I think too far beyond, I will collapse.

Emma is waiting in the attic when I come up from the shower. She is growing more lovely each time we meet. Perhaps it's the sadness. Someone to hold things up. She smiles, stands. Pulls me closer. My body is still damp. I lean into her, careful not to let my towel fall away. I back out. Kiss. Step into a small closet and dress. When I reemerge, Emma is lying on the bed. I join her and we stare at the slanted drywall. A spider casts shadows. Slanted and gray.

What should we do tonight, she asks.

Eat.

We lie like this a bit longer. I can feel her eyes on me. Boring a hole. Searching. I stare at the abutment of the top of the A frame. Emma pulls me to her. And then it's here. My body begins to fold in at the middle. My muscles contract. Tears at first and then sobbing.

Am I laughing? I ask.

You've never cried before?

Usually it's painful, I manage, like choking.

Emma pulls me closer and kisses my face. Where the tears stream. I attempt to pull away. It's too wet. Too something. She doesn't allow it. I continue my hybrid tearing. Before long, I stop. There is mucus in my throat. My nasal passage. Some other places hidden in my skull. Emma strokes my hair. She wraps her ankle over mine. She whispers sweet things, tells me she wishes I didn't hurt, that I didn't have to do this and that. When I feel her grip loosen, I slide free and stand. I attempt to flatten the wrinkles in my shirt.

✺

A series of rice dishes, faux meats, and Asian vegetables arrive at the dinner table. We scoop the food into our mouths. She, savoring; me, swallowing. My blood sugar is slow to rise. The world is fluorescent glares, clattering stainless steel, doors opening and closing. She looks at her food, her shoulders rolling in delight as she bends over to smell. She takes a bite and says things like "bad as shit" and "fucking good." I nod from time to time. I'm too hungry and shovel food into my mouth faster than I can chew it. I feel faint. I think of my father's glucose pills, how he had urged me to carry them with me as well. Beyond the veil, my father is teaching me lessons.

Emma's words begin emerging from the din of the room. Bits of them make sense but not enough that I can follow. I've learned well enough to act like I'm hearing other people when I'm not.

What do you mean? I ask.

Really?

Yes.

I mean, do you like your food?

I'm sorry. I misheard you because of the clamor of the room. Yes, it's fine.

Fine?

Yes.

So, you don't like it, she says in a tone that suggests it's a question. It's not a question.

Fine is good, I say.

No, fine is not good. Fine is what you say when you don't like something, but don't want to say it.

If I didn't like it, I would say it.

Emma chews on some rice, seemingly tired of the conversation. After a moment she says, we could have gone somewhere else.

Before I can analyze the words in my head, I say, I was fine with coming here.

Emma covers her mouth with a napkin as she begins laughing.

Look, I use fine in the same way I use it when describing a nice piece of furniture or a day. It's a fine day outside.

People don't say that, she says, putting more seitan on her fork. She then opens her hand, waves it before her and says, why, look what we have here, folks, a fine day, a fine day outside.

Maybe you're right, I muse. You've given me a fine example. Then I take a bite of noodles and say, asshole.

Emma lets it sit there, her eyes bright. She doesn't push it further, but I can see it fermenting in her craw. She laughs, but I know there's something else happening, something beneath the surface that's pulling the thing apart.

10

My father had gotten better. He'd been joking. The fog not so present in his eyes. We'd been moved into another room. A smaller room. Fewer machines. Less noise. The nurses not so attentive. We were waiting for the okay to move him to rehab. There was still a long road ahead of him. Months of physical therapy. I began looking for apartments in town. I didn't tell him this. I knew he wouldn't want me to move for him. He was sleeping as I browsed the classifieds. Looked at lofts. Sent emails to local universities inquiring about work. I knew it wasn't protocol. I wasn't following the rigid systemic process that kept faculty members safe from the world. Some responded with kindness. Others with condescension. Coldness.

My father had asked me some years ago to call on local universities and inquire about jobs. Use your moxie, he'd tell me. If only my father understood the complexities of the academic world. If only he knew that every year they wanted something more. More books. More essays. More awards. Then he would know that I was an unlikely candidate for most jobs. But in his eyes, I was infallible. At least it seemed that way to me. How does one tell a father the truth about himself? I looked from my screen. Watched him grasp at something in his sleep. I got up and lifted his sheet until his dreaming hand found it and grabbed hold. He pulled it to his chin. I looked at the monitor above him. Watched the lines pulse and shimmy. Watched the numbers drop and rise. What did it all mean? I began to organize his things. Pulled his wallet from his travel bag. Opened it. Half of his money had been taken by my brother. I pulled the big bills out. Hid them beneath his shoe insert. Sent a text to my sister. The money is in his left shoe.

My father opened his eyes. Smiled at me. I thought you went home, he said. No, I replied. Soon, sadly, soon. He made a face. Shifted his toothless mouth. Opened it. Lunch, he said, and almost as if he'd summoned it, the attendant wheeled the lunch cart into the hall. I laughed. Recalled the lazy summer days we'd simmer in the living room. Bored and watching reruns on television. He'd point to the phone and yell, ring. It never did. I always wanted it to. Hoped he'd summon some young thing to call me to her. To her suburban home with central air and cable television. Her parents bringing us cool drinks and chips.

When the attendant came, she didn't make eye contact. She placed the tray on his side table. I lifted the metal topper. Chicken. Mashed potatoes. A cookie. They're trying to kill me, he said. Yes, I agreed. I should take that cookie from you, I joked. He raised the fork as if to stab me.

11

A tug of skin over teeth. Down upon the cheek. Back around the scalp. This is how I look young again. Save for the hair. Thinning at the front. Widowing to a point. Myself in reverse. I push my hair this way. That. Power part. I tug at my ear lobe. Squint. Still I can't summon his ghost onto my face. Turning the overhead light off, switching on the nightlight—this helps. Hollows the eye sockets. I look more like him in shadows. And when I smile. The way my top lip curls. Exposes my teeth. Small moonstones. I lean in. Grimace. Tilt. Moan. In my father's voice, I say, every man has to shave sometime, Crag. I look at his shaving cream. His disposable razor. His aftershave. The same brand he's used since I can remember. Hi-Karate my father had called it. Smacking it on his cheeks. Dancing from the bathroom in a towel. Kick. Kick. Chop. Aye-Ya. I screw the top off. I dab a drop. Rub it between my fingers. Sniff. Putting it away, I see my father in the mirror. Only in passing. When I focus, he's gone. Staring at myself like some fool born to search. I laugh but it doesn't feel like laughing. A type of shallow coughing.

    The bathroom smells of mildew and piss. The places my father couldn't reach. Where he'd miss the john. Spray along the wall and down the side of the tub, the plunger and the corner. The urine doesn't come away easily. I spray it with cleaner. *Now with bleach! 30% more!* Letting it soak in, I sit on the toilet, my feet cocked on the rim of the tub, and read the paper. Local news. Other deaths. Weddings. Society page. Sports. Comics. I don't recognize any of the comics. When did they stop running comics I know? My voice against the tiles makes me feel like I'm suffocating. Or maybe it's the bleach.

This is the room where my father fell. Where he broke his hip while walking to piss. A type of crime scene. The body outlined in mildew. In urine. In new and improved cleaner.

I tug at the skin on my forearm. It clumps beneath my fingers and stretches into a sail when I lift. A release and it eases back into place. Not enough water. Never enough water. My vet once did this to my dog to show me that she was dehydrated because of a stomach thing—a bug or infection, I can't recall which. They put a needle beneath her skin and squeezed water between her flesh and muscle. Don't let your body go to shit, my father had warned me when I went to graduate school. I had listened, but now, measuring my own flesh in the room where my father fell, I wonder if I have been dedicated enough. Will the Diet Pepsi lead me down a path of no return? Will the lack of sleep? The bad posture?

The property manager comes to the door. I leave the urine to soak. We talk about the move-out date. She says she misses my father. Says he was like a father to her. Hands me a folded piece of paper and I thank her. It's only after she leaves that I unfold it. See it's a bill for damages. A way to treat a surrogate father, I say.

I collect my things and leave.

The children are leaving the middle school across the street. My sister is on the corner serving carpool duty. I don't want to talk to her. Dip behind a tree. Hear her yelling for a kid to be careful crossing the street. I push my back against the tree and shimmy forward until I'm sitting on the ground. Listen to the cars and kids and teachers and parents and dogs barking in the distance. The shade is nice, but the bole is hard against my spine.

12

When I left Louisville to return to work, my father had been cleared for release. They had moved him out of Intensive Care. He was waiting with a friend for an ambulance to move him. He was healthy. He was looking stronger. We had won.

By the time I landed, things had changed. My father's friend, Mary, had left a frantic message in which she claimed that the nurses had dropped him. They weren't supposed to move him, but they wanted to put him in a chair, so they could start cleaning the room for the next patient. Though my father had protested, arguing that he was far too heavy for them to lift alone, they did it anyway. When he began slipping out of their hands, one of the nurses simply let go and he hit the floor. Who does that? Mary shouted into my voicemail.

They left him writhing on the floor for fifteen minutes before two orderlies arrived. The doctor said he injured his hip again and tore his rotary cuff, she said, as if he'd done it on his fucking own.

I called Mary. I asked how he was doing. She said he was back ICU, that he wasn't well. He wasn't talking. Wasn't able to move parts of his body. She said that he was growing worse with every hour.

I called the hospital and spoke to a nurse. I asked what had happened. She looked at his notes and said that she didn't know. That maybe he fell out of his bed. There were no notes regarding the incident. Where are his doctors, I asked. They've gone home for the night, she said. My father was just in shock from the pain, she told me, He'll get better.

I worked as best I could. The end of the semester was upon me. I met with students. I apologized to them for my absence. I spent long hours in my office, helping them. My phone didn't ring. I called Mary; she didn't answer. As people do, I trusted everything was fine. If everything wasn't fine, I reasoned, someone would call me. I met with my department chair about a student complaint regarding my absences. I explained that she'd been failing long before I left town. She had yet to turn in work. Still, I reached out to her. Left messages. He said I would have to meet with the Dean to explain the situation.

The second night back home, I got another call from Mary. She said I should come back. She said, he's not looking good. She said that I should be there. I booked a flight for the following evening. It was the only ticket I could afford. The following morning, I received a call from my sister. She was crying. She told me that my dad's kidneys were failing, and Mary wanted me to give permission to take my father off of the machines that beeped and hummed. Mary wanted to take my father to hospice to die in peace. Mary told her that my father was talking to his mother's ghost. My sister asked me to come home and make the decision because she couldn't bear it.

I changed my flight. It wasn't something I could afford. I had to call my credit card company. Beg them for a small increase. I called the department chair and told him I had to go.

On the flight, I looked at photos of my father. I wanted to cry. I wanted to be the stranger on the plane weeping. The one who felt things. Instead I just looked at his face. I mapped the similarities between us. I thought of the things he had done for me. My heart became a warm stone.

When I arrived, he had a sleep apnea mask on. He was yellow and frail. Mary, Karen, and my sister stood around him, whispering. They looked like witches from some cartoon from long ago, all gathered there in shadow. My sister rushed to me. She pleaded with me. She called the other women angels of death. They want to kill him, she said. I can't make the decision, she said. I asked them all to leave the room. I sat in a chair beside my father. I pulled his hand into mine. I kissed it. I stroked it softly. The medical tape crinkled beneath my thumb. He looked at me. His eyes were wild. He opened his mouth in a child-like smile. His dentures were out. I told him that I loved him. I asked him if he knew that. He nodded. This gave me hope. I looked him in his eyes. I asked a question I'd never imagined I'd ask: do you want to die? He mouthed something round. Squeeze my hand, I said, if you want to go to hospice. He did not. Squeeze my hand if you want to fight and live. He squeezed my hand. With his free hand, he tried to point to the mask. I unhooked it. It was not easy. I was worried the elastic bands would snap free. Would sting him with their whip. I pulled the plastic away. Already the machine began beeping. He mouthed something to me with a fricative. I said, you want to live. He nodded. I slipped his mask back on. I fastened it. I kissed his forehead.

As I began to walk away, he touched my hand. I let him pull mine into his. He shook it as tightly as he could and smiled.

When I entered the hallway, I told the women that he wanted to live. That he spoke to me. They were surprised. They asked if I wasn't just thinking he did. I said that I was not just thinking. The nurse walked into the room as we spoke. She came back out and said, he's urinated. Then she said, he waved to me. My sister hugged me. She said that I brought him back. Mary seemed conflicted. I saw doubt finger her wrinkled skin.

Soon after, everyone left. I sat in the dim room with my father, and watched his chest rise and fall, again. The movements were much slighter. He was on the precipice between this world and the next. I would not stop watching. I would will it to continue. This is what it is to care, I told myself. We sit by our loved ones and will breath into them. We reseal the door between worlds. We cast furtive glances at the shadowy corners to ensure no family spirits call to them. We eat candy bars from vending machines for dinner and drink cola. We lose track of days and nights and sleep upright. We learn to ignore the clamor of machines and read books in the near-dark.

II

INFECTION

13

The day before the funeral I take a break from clearing out my father's apartment. There are still mountains of things to be sorted. I haven't the energy. My siblings never come. One is too busy with work. The other too sad to help. I drive to visit Emma. The drive is therapeutic. The green hills undulating. The limestone cliffs threatening collapse. The lakes and rivers. I listen to music. Something modern with dull synth pads, echoing vocals, driving bass. The world seems possible in a car. Everything streams by and I am safe.

 When I arrive at Emma's, she is late to the door. Something about her lab. Something about a table. She had studied science and linguistics and film. I can't remember in what order. She loves the math of language; I love the sound. We are able to talk about language, but at some point, she steers the conversation into an area in which I have little interest. Once she said: for a writer, you're terrible with words. She often jokes about my disinterest in what she calls the science of language. Emma opens the door and lets me inside. The house still smells of paint. I don't tell her this. Instead, I give her a hug. I go into the living room and sit on the couch. It's new. Cushions with little give. I adjust but find no comfort. I stare at the mid-century coffee table. At the bends in the legs, the look that made Pearsall tables so desirable. I wonder if I'll ever make enough to afford a two-thousand-dollar table. Emma likely found it at an estate sale. Some mourning descendent unaware of its value—just some old thing their mom had kept too long. I don't have her patience. Her eye. Her skill. The way she combs through piles of trash to save one relic. One perfect thing that won't be erased from the world. Sometimes I wonder if I am some such thing.

On the table is a small white label with the word *table* printed on it. I almost ask about it but notice that the television has a tag as well. Everything has a tag. *Wall, window, bookcase, book, speaker.* Emma notices me reading the tags.

It's the first stage, she says.

In what?

Recognizing the sign.

This, I understand. I see the signs. Understand the signifiers. What's the second step, I ask.

Oh shit, there's a lot of steps, but the next step is listing origins and then locating the connection.

Isn't language arbitrary?

No, Emma says, passion in her voice, strong and edged. That's a misconception.

That's dependent upon the school of linguistics you subscribe to, though.

She smiles and says, I'm looking for the biological sign.

What do you mean exactly?

Does a bull know language?

No.

Yet, a bull knows the color red.

But is that language?

Exactly, that's the biological sign. It possesses a communicating factor without the use of spoken or written language. I am looking for the natural meaning.

Emma's eyes gloss over as she speaks. A lighted glee in

her expression that I've never seen before. She speaks and she's in a trance. She speaks of natural signs and morphology. The more language she uses the more emphatic the joy in her expression. She has a very similar look during lovemaking. When she talks to me of her love. When she drinks her favorite smoothie. It once occurred to me that these are her primal joys and now I see that the study of language brings her this same joy. Perhaps more, because her eyes seem near bursting when she stops. I don't know if it's logical or possible or a theory without any scientific grounding. I just see how happy it makes her. I reason that's good enough for me.

I'm boring you.

I say, no. I like the way you light up when you talk about it.

I don't want to show my hand. Reveal my ignorance in her world. Part of me wants to say it's all bullshit, but another part of me is just scared of looking stupid. What would happen if I turn out to be less intelligent than she thought? Would I still be that Pearsall in the rubbish? Or something else entirely?

She says, but you think that the science of language subtracts from the beauty and mystery, I know...We don't have to talk about this. We can get lunch.

Emma takes my hand into hers. Is this mercy? She calls Chelsea, puts a collar on her, fastens a leash. The pit bull is beside herself with joy. Jumps. Yips. Trimmed tail tremoring. Chelsea comes to me. Paws on my lap. Tongue flimsy out her mouth. Emma is in the bathroom. Inspecting herself in the mirror. She's wiping small things from around her eyes. Makeup that has flaked from her lashes. Things I'm blind to. I rub my fingers on the small loaves of meat between Chelsea's ears. She is trusting for a rescue. Sweet. I wonder if Zelda and Chelsea will get along; dogs can be so unpredictable. I'd always been a cat person, but Zelda fell in my lap. So adorable with her goofy paws and mismatched eyes, a puppy most irresistible. It's always been easy for me to love animals. People take work. They're secrets waiting to explode. Animals just want love.

We leave the gentrified block, where the mid-century homes that had been abandoned in the eighties, have been restored and sit, sleek and cutting upon the hill, their yards kempt, green, and flawless, and descend a street into a neighborhood with children playing. There are a dozen or so. All playing with sun faded plastics: Big wheels, baseball bats, street cones. Their black skin wet with sweat. The sun reflecting off them like burning fleshy stars. Emma walks fast, Chelsea slightly faster. Leash taut. It terrifies me to watch the dog so close to the edge of traffic. Emma, full hipped and slender waisted, holds the leash steady. She is in the wrong year. The wrong decade. She matches her dress and house and music to the time she wishes she'd been born in. Atomic age. Baby booms. Yet, still manages to survive the aughts. I wonder if she had lived back then, if she'd still have the same fierce personality she has now, saving the beautiful things others want to destroy. I haven't been so dedicated to a look. To a time. I've cobbled things together. My house a museum of curiosities. Contemporary and antique. I wonder what is crazier: the streamlined or the chaotic? Chelsea picks up a piece of cat shit. She devours most of it before Emma can stop her. I laugh.

It's not funny, she jokes, wait until she licks you.

Emma crosses the road. She said the restaurant was around the block. It's been twenty minutes since we left the house. I remember the phrase: a country mile. I remember walking to get candy as a child. I remember being in New York and walking, walking, walking. I'm hungry. My blood sugar low. I begin to fall behind. Chelsea continues to pull Emma along at a driving pace. Emma is unaware that I'm a half block back, but I don't say anything. Wander at a casual pace. Look at the houses. The shotgun homes next to the decaying Victorians. Front yard bathtubs with weeds bursting out of them. Bottles of liquor resting in the abutment of stone walls and sidewalks. Candy wrappers tangled in nettle bushes. Chain link fences with "beware of dog" signs. One with a "fuck the dog, beware of owner" sign, a handgun printed at the bottom. A wind blows but it's no respite from the heat.

Woah, Chelsea, Emma says. She looks back at me. She smiles. Tilts her head. Her bangs rigid. Straight along her eyebrows. I catch up. She asks if I'm okay. I tell her that I like to walk slowly. To take things in. She locks arms with me. The sweat in the crux of her arm mingles with mine. I kiss her shoulder. I know her sweat. Know the taste of it. She doesn't know this. She doesn't know that her body gives her away. That I know her pleasure before she tells me. Doesn't know that when I say love, I mean the planets seen and unseen, the burning stars, the weight of everyone's lungs, the end of time—forever and ever, amen.

We arrive at the café and order. I get eggs and faux sausage. Sometimes I wonder if it bothers her. The taste of egg in my mouth. If kissing me makes her skin crawl. On the sundeck, we dine beneath a grand blue umbrella. Chelsea tries to lick my hand. I move it just in time. Put it in my lap like some pioneer holding a gun. Emma makes sounds while she eats. Talks about how good it is. This is what she does. She knows pleasure. It's frequent. Perhaps that part of my brain is damaged. Perhaps I don't feel pleasure the way others do.

What do you consider fun? I ask.

Emma stops chewing for a moment. She looks at me. Her eyes glinting in the shaded sunlight. A blink. Are you serious, she asks.

Yes.

I find fun in everything, she says, I don't let myself get bored.

When do you feel sad, I ask.

I don't want to talk about sadness. I see it. But I don't want to talk about it. She looks at me, cocks her head, says, your depression worries me. Touching the cut of my jaw with her fingers, she lights up a little, but it's not the light of joy. It's something else, something akin to pity.

Don't worry.

Your sadness fills rooms, she says, I can feel it now.

We're not in a room.

Don't be cute.

I have a reason to be sad.

I know. But even when you don't have a reason.

I want to say something about reasons. I want to ask for a list of approved reasons. I know better. Emma escalates. She explodes. She gets fixated on her rightness and can't see otherwise. But she also doesn't mean to be cruel. She means something else. To end this thing that fills me. She doesn't see sadness as a virus. She sees it as something to switch off. Something that I can choose not to experience.

Do I make you happy, she asks.

Yes, I say.

Mostly, I think.

We leave and begin the walk back. It seems shorter. Hunger made it seem a longer way. Unfamiliarity. A group of children runs around the corner in a game of chase. They stop short of Emma and the dog. They recoil. The younger of the boys wrings the bottom of his yellow tank top in his fingers. Ma'am, he says, that dog scary.

A taller boy asks, you fight him?

Emma says, no. Fighting dogs is a terrible thing to do. Chelsea is a sweetheart.

The taller boy replies, those dogs are mean.

Emma offers the children a chance to pet the dog. They decline. Chelsea approaches one. Curious. The boy screams and the lot of them run back up the hill and over the horizon. Emma doesn't move. She stares at Chelsea. She touches the dog. She says something to herself that I can't hear. I ask her what she said. She doesn't respond. She's in a trance. She's thinking about work. She's solving a problem. I can see it. Her eyes. They seem to inch out, to widen. Emma pulls at a loose fold of Chelsea's neck. The dog licks her and Emma snaps to.

Ready, she asks. Her voice a joyful octave higher.

14

I went to my father's apartment and gathered a few of his things. I grabbed some clothes. His slippers. I brought his bamboo back scratcher. The bag was filling quickly. Glasses. Hat. Cell phone. When I arrived back at the hospital, I worried something had happened that my sibling had neglected to write down. My brother had taken a few dollars out of my father's wallet and written a note on the journal: I love my dad. Nothing else.

Did they do his breathing treatments, I asked a nurse. She said they hadn't. She told me that my father had pneumonia, that she had told my brother. She brought me a device. It looked like a small drink pitcher with a bendy straw. She put the straw in my father's mouth, she told him to blow. He sucked. She said, no, I want you to blow. He sucked. She asked again and still he sucked. I took the device. I said, buddy, watch me. I put it in my mouth. I could taste his tacky saliva on the end, stale crackers and death. I blew. Several blue balls rattled on the inside and a needle lifted along a ruler. See, I told him, blow not suck. I wiped the straw clean. Placed it in his mouth. He sucked at first then stopped and reversed. The balls barely moved. Again, the nurse said. Again, he tried. He began coughing. Wet. Wet. Wet. Good, she said.

My father seemed to nod off and clicked his tongue against the roof of his mouth. He clapped his lips. My mouth is so dry, he said. He held his tongue out as far as he could. I'd never seen a tongue go white from dehydration. I asked the nurse for water. She told me he couldn't drink until he urinated more. She said he was too bloated. That it was affecting his pneumonia. I said his mouth is white. That he is unhappy. That I was worried. She brought me a cup with ice water and a small sponge on the end of a wire. It looked like a pipe cleaner with all of its bristles pushed to the end. I asked my father to open his mouth. I said, buddy, open your mouth and suck on this sponge. He did as I asked. He sucked and moaned as if it was the greatest pleasure he'd known. I removed it and he attempted to say, *more.* I dabbed the sponge back into the cup. A fine chalky mist blossomed in the water. I repeated feeding him water through a tiny sponge. Each time I did it, the water grew murkier. I wondered what it would be like to drink from the cup. How quickly I would vomit. I felt bad feeding him dirty water. Even though it was from his mouth, it felt wrong. I drained it, rinsed the cup, filled it. Started again. Each time to the same results.

The memory of my father waking me as a child to break my fever arose. He would hold me as he rubbed me down with cool water. He would bring me a cold glass of Gatorade. He would clean the vomit from my wastebasket. He would give me a change of clothes. He would change my sheets. Leave the television on cartoons in case I woke up again.

When I'd finished giving him water, I told my father I loved him. I told him this every time he woke up. I didn't want him to fall into death without having heard me say it before closing his eyes.

My father coughed—wet. I could hear his breath rattling in his throat. I struggled to clear my mine as if this would help him.

He turned to me, the light from the hallway tracing his body. Some artificial sunrise. He lifted his hand and pointed to his mask. I undid the straps. Pulled it free. He motioned for me to sit. I did.

You, he whispered, you are the one who can hold this all together.

I was surprised by his lucidity. I saw it as a good sign. I said, okay.

It was always you, he said, who kept it together. I love you, he said.

I love you too, Dad.

These people are trying to kill me, he managed. You, he said and paused.

Yeah, buddy, I said.

He continued to pause then said, I think I'm going to piss. He looked at me with a tender expression I'd scarcely seen. No, he said, no, I'm shitting myself.

It's okay, dad. I said. I can get a nurse and we'll clean you up.

No, he said, wait.

I waited.

You're my son. You have to hold it together. You have to make sure they don't kill me. You have to promise me that. He paused again and said, if I die…

You're not going to die, Dad.

If I die, you can't take care of your brother and sister. You can't be their dad. Promise me, he said, his voice fading, promise me that you'll stay away if I die.

I stood up, weakened by the stench of his waste. I grabbed his hand. I promise, buddy. Let's clean you up.

I switched on the lights. They flickered and faded up, their unforgiving luminosity hammering my head, softening my stomach. I notified a nurse. She and an orderly came in to clean my father. I assisted. I'd been sitting in his room for so long feeling helpless. I slipped on gloves, held my breath, used a warm damp rag to scoop away yellow waste that had spread to his back. I parted his buttocks. I wiped away the waste between. Stealing breaths a few feet away, I came back each time with less strength. I cleared him and toweled him dry. The nurses changed the bedding. My father moaned in pain. He was on his side. His back and ass exposed through the gown. When they finished, they lay him back down. He'd grown used to it. He sniffed a few times, cleared his throat. He tried to fold his hands but fell asleep just shy of the connection.

After a few hours passed, the nice nurse came in. She asked why my father was back in ICU. I explained what had happened. She seemed angry. She seemed to take it personally. She said some nurses were not very good at their jobs. She said that some nurses became nurses because of the demand. She handed me a care package. It contained rubber gloves, some snacks, and a small bottle of cheap body spray. The latter was to spray my father. To help assuage the smell in the room. I thanked her and went to the sink to clean up.

It wasn't long after that she returned in a yellow gown. She called me outside. Pointed to a stack of boxes on a chair. She explained to me that we'd have to wear gowns, masks, and gloves until he was released. My father had MRSA; he was contagious. This, she said, is a bad development. That my father was now fighting for his life.

I dressed and returned. My breath stifled by the mask. I sat by my father's side. As I watched him struggle to breathe, his body struggling to release water, I began to think about what he'd said. I thought about my siblings. How little they'd been there. I had always felt guilty for being away during his other health scares, but took comfort that they'd been there, though I would learn that they had not. They buckled under the stress, always turning the reigns over to my cousin or my father's friends. Again, a finger of guilt pushed inside me and then something popped and I was angry—angry at myself, angry at the doctors, angry at my siblings.

I understood that this was all counter-productive, but there it was, caught in my throat, a denticulate mass, cutting as it burrowed deeper. I took as deep a breath as I could. Relaxed it. Focused on my breathing until I felt the tension slipping away. I knew my brother and sister felt like I'd abandoned my father by living across the country, and though troublesome thoughts stung at me repeatedly, I dashed them away with memories of my father.

I opened my computer and began searching for videos of an interview that I'd conducted with my father the previous year. We'd sat across from one another in his living room. The pill bottles between us. I'd asked him questions. He'd answered. He said he'd been trying to tell his stories to my brother for years. That my brother never listened. I didn't know this to be true. After all, my brother often picked up more than we thought he did. I asked my father about his mother. I asked him about his first love. About his childhood and his history playing football. He answered all my questions. When I asked him about his career, he lit up. Work was his legacy. It was the one thing that made him happy.

In silence, I watched as my father sat hunched over in a chair by his dinner table. He was wearing a red and black checked shirt and a ball cap pulled low over his eyes. He was shy but steady. I wanted to listen to the sound but couldn't find my headphones. When I finished, I watched him sleep.

I thought of the tragedy of it all. A man who had been swindled out of millions, who had fallen into drink only to sober up twenty years later when he was too old to work. A man who had been beloved and chose to hide because he was too prideful to let people see him living in poverty. What would they say all these years later? Would they come here and apologize for swindling from him, those friends whom he'd held so dear?

Would they whisper that they would pay the bills, visit more often, repay him for his kindness?

I placed my hand on my father's. It was strange not feeling his skin. I stroked his knuckles. The latex or plastic or whatever it was caught at times. It pulled at him. It bunched under my touch. Felt inhuman. Even with me in the room, I felt like my father was isolated again.

15

Emma is standing by her window. She has pulled the sheet off the bed. She is folding it. Boxes. Tighter and tighter. She folds until it cannot fold any further, then places it on a table. She returns to the bed. Pulls the cover off her pillow and returns to the window. She folds it. When it can fold no more, she places it on the sheet.

I stand and watch. I wonder what other strange things she does in her sleep. I wonder if she eats or dances or paints or writes emails. If she'll wake up without me saying anything? Emma returns to the bed and begins pulling the fitted sheet off the mattress. I watch as she unfastens the top left corner. The bottom left. When she gets to my side, I ask, are you having a night terror?

Emma replies, no.

What are you doing?

I'm clearly, she says, I'm obviously...She trails off for a moment, seems to search the room with her eyes. Yes, she says, yes. She crawls back onto the bed and wraps herself in the fitted sheet.

I walk into the hallway and stare back at Chelsea, who sleeps at the foot of the bed. Sometimes, when Emma showers, Chelsea crawls into bed with me. She knows she's breaking the rules. She knows it's wrong. She crawls under the sheets to hide. Spoons me. Puts a leg over my chest.

Blows warm breath into my ear. When I hear Emma leave the shower, I'll get up and call Chelsea to the dog bed, kiss her on her head. Sometimes, though, we are caught. Sometimes I fall back to sleep. The hot sun cutting into my face. The dog's belly warming my side.

I walk to the living room, sit on the hard sofa, and look at all the things with their labels. The world on a grid. There is something unsettling about it. All the clean lines. Something about the ease of it. Something about the ease of perfections. Something in me is tempted to move things. To switch labels. To see how long it would take her to discover. I do nothing. I will do anything to hurt her. Not intentionally. I know that inevitably I will. I know it's the price of a life. Hurting the ones I love. That everyone does it.

Light burns along the seams of small lead window frames in hot blue lines. It's blinding and saddening to watch the sunrise. It's a reminder of life, which is a reminder of death. The birds fly to their nests. They make noises. The garbage trucks backfire. The neighbor's kids run out the back door, letting the screen door slam.

It seems I'm always watching garbage trucks. My insomnia always forcing me on the edge of night and day. I remember watching a fluorescent green truck cresting a distant hill outside Stuttgart. It stopped every few minutes to gather trash, its hazard light blinking yellow in the early mist. My motorcycle had died in the night and I'd tried to find town without success. In a thicket of frozen grass, I unrolled my sleeping bag and tried to sleep until day came and I could flag down an ADAC truck or find my way to a phone. It seems no coincidence now that I attempted to write a postcard to Emma then, all those years ago, to confess my unspoken feelings, that I'd often thought of a life with her before I fell to sleep at nights, and again no coincidence that I lost that card before sending it. Some things must wait.

Then, just as now, I hated watching the garbage men, their day in full swing as mine had been obscured into a fog of sleeplessness. I envy those who find sleep so easily. Those who can keep schedules and have productive lives.

Emma stirs. She speaks my name. Crag, she says. I want to answer but feel my mouth seal. Crag, she says. The second time I reply. The second time I say that I'm still here. I say that I'm in the living room. I hear the suction of her feet on the floor. Feel her presence in the living room. She is on me. Her arms wrapped loosely around my neck.

What happened to the bed, she asks.

You undid it, I say.

Is that why you're in here?

No, I lie. Then say, I'm here to watch the sun rise. I'm here to watch life.

Emma kisses my cheek. I love it when you're positive, she says. She leaves and goes to the bathroom.

I look at the labels fastened to the glass tabletop. I pick at one with my toenail. Stop just shy of pulling it free. I'll go back soon. I'll finish cleaning the apartment. I'll unsettle my father's things. I'll break chairs and put them in a dumpster. I'll give things to the other residents. They will wait outside the apartment like buzzards on a highway.

✺

I outline a cleaning plan on my drive home. I forget music. Forget phones exist. I only see the post death tasks before me. The giving. The throwing. The shattering. The collecting. Then I lose track of it. I become a moment of passing. Skies and hills and blooms. Highways snaking and curling. Points where they eat their own tails. Moments where trucks move too slowly. At times I find myself tapping. Some abstracted beat. Perhaps a song from childhood. A dirge of fingers. I think of Juliana. Of our time together. The time before the falling and taking and giving. Before Emma took me into her arms. I don't know why I edit this narrative from Emma. Why I remove Juliana's name from stories. I'm aware that I'll never know how much I edit until later. One day I may think about it. I might lie in a bedroom alone thinking of Emma and thinking of Juliana. Alone without either. Two narratives that will likely end too soon. It is a thing lovers do. A thing people do when moments are fragile. When they're already on their second chance. Instinctual. Protective. Dig in so deep it's impossible to remember the truth.

And what of the other? Of Juliana looking after the dog. She too is precious. But we both understood that the end is to come sooner or later. I reasoned sooner than later. We can manage communication. We still watch movies. Still see sunsets. Still laugh. This is how I see it. It doesn't sway. I break my chain of thought, pull off the highway, and drive toward my father's house. I could have hit someone. Killed a deer. There is no end to what could have transpired in-between my leaving and now. Time lost to thought. I wouldn't have been prepared for it. No one thinks of this when they drive. No one says, I need to stop thinking lest I kill someone. Something. And if I did? It too would become my work. A part of a book. Loss is my business and I've never been so aware of it until now. Everything seems out of reach. The ideas that usually occupy me are scarce. Death it seems is only available when I'm living at a distance. When I'm too close, it hides. Instead of writing, I sit and stare. At a wall. At a car. At a bee crawling a bloom. There's no real thought, just faded ideas. When close, death occupies me in a different way. It calls me to action and strikes language nearly whole from me.

Along the streets, the trash cans bake beneath the sun, the smell of each unique but sharing the same characteristics of things putrefying. The heat radiates from the road in ghosting waves and distant traffic is made blurry by them. The city has freshly tarred the cracks in the road and the protective sand they'd scattered on top has mostly gone to waste. When stopping at lights, the car has trouble staying cool.

At the home, there is a circle of old women by the door. There is a type of chittering. A sound of crickets with rusty legs. One says she's sorry for my loss. Words obscured in the folds flesh and tarry mucus. I thank her. Turn the first security key. The second. On the other side of the doors is the apartment manager. She has forms. She has deadlines. She requests money to pay for cleaning the carpets, white washing, a broken shelf. I take the papers. Say I understand. Walk to the elevator and begin the slow ascent to the third floor. In the hallway, I toss the paperwork into the trash.

I'm surprised to see my sister at the front door. She's writing a note. Leaning against the door. Scribbling. I call her name. She stops, turns.

Shit. I was going to leave you a note.

Okay, I say.

I can't help today. Dwayne doesn't feel like coming with his truck.

I nod and slip by her to unlock the door. I open it so that my sister can see what's left. The smell of my father's life rushes out. My sister is on the verge of crying; it's a bulge in the throat that pulls her head down and distorts her voice.

I can't help today, she says, I have to go home. Dwayne said maybe tomorrow.

Maybe tomorrow, I repeat for no reason but to keep from

saying something about Dwayne. About Dwayne's absence during the hospital visits. His absence during the mourning period. About his absence from anything that would require those actions which are inherently human. To prevent myself from saying anything about his addiction to this or that. I say, if he can't come soon, I'll call Salvation Army to pick everything up.

But that's dad's stuff, she pleads.

Yes.

She twitches her lips in a pout. Okay, she says, I'll make him come.

I say goodbye and return to undoing things. I do this until every trash bag is full. I don't speak a word for hours. Don't answer the door. Don't heed the skeletal knuckles upon the wood. The begging old waiting for things. I stop occasionally to drink a cool glass of water. To eat a generic yoghurt from my father's fridge. When the room grows too hot, I chip away the pile of ice cubes my father created in the freezer. When I grow tired, I rest on a footlocker and read clippings from his high school and college papers. My father had always been a social creature. His wild antics and athleticism attracted the school papers. He once told me he'd broken into a professor's office and stolen the answers for the test so his football team would all pass the class. He told the story with a sense of pride. When I finish an article about his performance at a fraternity choir performance I have to stop reading as it feels as if my heart is so full of sadness that it might burst. I go to the bathroom mirror and search for my father's ghost. It does not greet me.

As the last hem of sunlight dips below the treeline, I leave the building. There are bugs calling. I don't know what kind. I likely know some of the names. Most I don't. A voice calls after me as I traverse the parking lot. It's frail and old and begging. I feign deaf. I continue my sluggish walk. My shoulders lowered from hunger. My head sore from heat. These two blocks are filled with song lyrics. They come, invisible and potent. They remind me of my father in bed. The feeble last days. The static in the hospital air.

Emma is on the steps. I don't see her at first. It isn't until Chelsea jumps on me that I return to the world. I stumble back. My heartbeat heavy, hard. Exhausted, I allow the momentum to grow. Fall upon the grass. Allow the dog to topple me, to lick my face. Emma joins us. She kisses my face, still wet from the dog. This is a moment. This is a thing I will remember. I lean my head against Emma's shoulder. She asks if I'm hungry. I try to nod. I try to speak.

What's open, I ask finally.

What time is it, she asks.

Where's my phone, I say.

Try your pocket, she says.

I pull my phone out to check the time. I'm unaware of the messages until it's too late. Juliana. Juliana. Juliana. Juliana. Juliana. It's as if the air has gone flat, or there's a shift in the earth's movement, everything in a strange minor key. I shut the phone off. I try to act like it hasn't happened. I say the time. I say the time like Emma didn't see what I'd seen. I say, ten o'clock. I repeat it in a breathy whisper. It's my fault. I should know better. I'm tired. Several minutes go by without a response from Emma.

I want to tell Emma a joke. It's about a man in a bar. It involves some strange event or character or pun. I want to share it with her but won't. I know it's ill-advised. That her temper is quick. My feelings too frail. Instead, I tell the joke to the dog. The dog blinks at me. Slowly. No one laughs.

Emma is staring at me, her gaze a hot finger on my temple. I don't say anything. I pet the dog and stare at the tree branches.

Aren't you going to read it?

No.

Why not?

Because I'm fucking tired, Emma.

Emma says, what the fuck. It is a declarative and not a question. Why does she need to contact you so many times, she asks. She sits up and says, this is sketch.

What is?

You are. You're sketchy as shit.

Why am I sketchy?

I've asked my friends and they agree.

Asked your friends, I say, sitting up somewhat.

About your dog sitter, Emma says stressing the final words. She doesn't like to call Juliana by her name. It's as if naming her is a validation. Is something up with her, she asks.

No.

You can tell me. Now is the time to tell me. Don't tell me later. You know honesty is important to me. It's *the* most important thing to me.

There is nothing going on with me and Juliana.

Nothing at all.

No, nothing is going on right now.

Emma seems okay with this. I've bought time. I've told the truth. Part of a bigger truth. It's not a lie. I'm not misleading Emma. There are parts of my life that do not pertain to her. There are parts of me that are mine. Private things that are not meant for her to share. Memories and stories that do not belong to everyone.

16

Once my father told me a joke. The joke goes like this:

A radio news reporter is out in the field polling voters as they leave voting stations. He approaches a man and asks him if he voted. The man says, yes. The reporter asks him who he voted for. The man replies, Argo. The reporter laughs and says, Argo, who is Argo? The man says, Argo fuck yourself. The reporter is fired. Years later, after working his way back into live reporting, the correspondent is given the task of interviewing people attending a comedy festival and asking them their favorite knock-knock joke. As he makes his way through the crowd, he finds himself interviewing the man who'd cost him his job. The man says, knock-knock. The reporter asks, who's there? The man replies, Mary. The reporter thinks quickly and can't think of any possible inappropriate responses and asks, Mary who? The man smiles and says, Argo fuck yourself.

I stared at my father. He finished his breathing exercises. He managed to get his arms moving some. This is a good thing, I told myself. He was gaining his strength. He was staring at the TV. There was a reporter talking about the Derby week.

Emma called and asked if she could see my father. I wasn't

sure what to say so I said sure. When she arrived, my father was asleep. It didn't seem right to have someone so full of life in that room. She looked placed, some digital sleight of hand where they put a flower in a catacomb. Emma suggested we take a walk. It'd be good for me, she said. We made our way through the city, visiting hat shops. We tried on ridiculous Derby hats and laughed. Just as I'd put on a seven-hundred-dollar number, a saleswoman came to us and asked if we were planning on buying anything. We left and went to Broadway, where the Pegasus Parade began.

In the parking lot of a fast food restaurant, we sat on a low brick wall and watched as marching bands, floats, and large Pegasus balloons passed. A couple of high school kids necked beside us. In that moment, the late afternoon sun warm on my back, the world breathed and my flesh shuddered in pleasure.

As the final marching band played its way past us, the sun fell behind the glassy skyline, and in those shadows, I felt the word *father* upon my tongue. He was in his hospital bed. I should have been there. I shouldn't have left. I should have been a better son. His friend was relieving me of my duties. I felt like I was failing him. Like when I moved away. When I never moved back.

He asked me what time it was when I returned. I told him. He asked again. I gave the same answer. He asked me if he'd already asked me. I said, it's okay, buddy. You're tired. You need your rest, I said. You're getting much better, I said.

Inside I longed for it to be over. For my father to be well. I longed for the days when I'd visit and sit across the table from him.

When he'd fall asleep sitting up in his chair. When the clock on the wall seemed to tick louder with each passing minute. I would watch him sleep, his neck craned forward. I would ask him to get into bed. I would ask him to sleep on the couch at least. I'd ask him to sit back in the recliner. He would always refuse. He was tough.

In the notes, my father's friend wrote that he'd asked to join his mommy (I wondered if this was his word choice or hers). That he'd said he was tired. Did he really want to die? What if he was just putting on a brave face for me? The way parents do. To look strong. He'd do this. When I'd visited him in rehab after his fall, after his infection, I'd walked in as he was bouncing a ball with a physical therapist. She said he could quit, but he said, no. He waved for her to throw the ball again. He looked like he was competing. She bounced the ball. He caught it and bounced it back. I was proud of him. He wanted me to see how strong he was—his way of taking worry off of my shoulders.

The nurse came in and asked my father how he was doing. My father said, Argo. I laughed. He smiled. It was a child's smile. Playful and toothless. The black in his mouth seemed so vast. He held it. Perhaps too long. Then it faded and he looked at his hands as if they were not his own. He turned them in the light. He rubbed them together. The nurse asked what Argo meant. I told her it was Greek for better. She remarked that she learned something new every day at work. She prodded my father. She needled him for blood. His arms were ripe with bruises. She said that she was having trouble getting a vein. She poked at him more. Goddamn it, my father said, pulling his arm away in an other-worldly creep. She called in another nurse. An older nurse. She came in and attempted. It took time, but she got it. Then she said he needed a port. I asked what that was. She explained that it was something that would stay in one place and they could hook him to different IVs and such things. I said, like a break out box. She said, what? I said it again. I know she didn't understand what I meant, but she said, yes, and left the room. The first nurse adjusted my father's pillow. When she finished, she asked him, Argo? He did not reply.

My father was tired. I could see it in him. He fought but he wanted to be left alone, but they wouldn't leave him alone. I thought about how horrible it must be. Being trapped in that bed. How they came to him constantly. How I got a few breaks to sleep or eat or see people or see trees. My father didn't have that choice. He saw the same things. The same people. The same pricking, prodding, flipping, and disturbing every hour. A doctor came to the door. He didn't speak to me. He looked at my father from the doorway. He read a chart.

Who are you, I asked. He didn't answer me. I walked to him and he stepped back. He was Indian or Pakistani. His peach suit was bright against his skin. Who are you, I asked. What are you looking at? He mumbled something that I couldn't discern.

I learned later that he was the doctor who was monitoring my father's infection. He did not care to speak with me. He was not humane or kind. He seemed annoyed at the fact that I should talk to him, question him. His reluctance fueled my insistence. I began to ask more questions. He tried to walk away from me. I followed him. A nurse called to me. She told me I couldn't wear my robes out of the room. I asked the doctor to come into the room, to see my father. He said he had other patients to attend to. The nurses came to me. They pressured me to return to the room. In the moment I looked to them, the doctor had vanished.

I wrote in my father's journal. I wrote the man's name. Then I wrote, doctor asshole. For the duration of the journal, I would refer to him as doctor asshole.

I was reminded of my mother's death.

We'd agreed not to resuscitate her in the likely event of her death. When I told the nurse that my mother had stopped breathing, she called the doctor. He came in and took her pulse. He asked if we wanted to resuscitate her. I saw the change of heart forming on my father's face. I said, no, we do not. The doctor said, well then, she's dead. He turned around and began walking out of the room. He said it as if it weren't the end of a life. As if he was annoyed that we'd asked him to come into the room. There was no sympathy in his voice, no human register. My arm pulled back, a fist balled. Had my sister not fallen upon me crying, I would have punched him. It was not a thought I had. It was not as if I thought, and now I will punch the doctor. My body just reacted. I'm lucky my sister hugged me. Dumb luck.

I didn't want to punch the doctor in the peach suit. I was older. Less prone to those indiscretions of youth. However, I did want to make him uncomfortable. I wanted him to know that he was not above my father or me. That he would talk to us like equals.

I wanted my father to have the best health care available but he was on public assistance. He was registered as a charity case. They gave him the best care they could give but we were by no means at the best hospital in the city.

Over the years, my father learned to work the system. He'd figured out how to get the best medical care, the best food, the best senior insurance, the best everything for the little he received in Social Security. I think it bothered me more than him that his lifetime of hard work, where he should have been retiring in some warm resort town, was only rewarded with loss and poverty. I should have been there for him. Given him a home when his world fell apart. When he was living in squalor on the farm. But I didn't know. I was across the country. I was racking up debt at universities. He said he was proud of me, but I didn't feel good about it. Certainly not then. Not looking at my frail father in his hospital bed. I should have been able to pay for better health care. I should have been a better son.

17

My brother had called me from my father's phone. It caught me off guard, seeing my father's phone number again gave me some strange sense of hope, as if it all had been a terrible misunderstanding and my father was actually still alive. I answered with hesitation and, upon hearing my brother's voice, tried as best I could to level my tone, chase the brackish mist of anger from my tongue. My brother is coping with this too.

    I am sitting at a table on the sidewalk. It's near a private college and classes have just ended. The lacrosse team already drunk and drinking more beer by the pitcher. The waitress brings me a soda water with a pale slice of lime fizzing between the ice cubes. Not surprised by my brother's tardiness, I sip my drink and look at the pansies hanging beside me. I stroke the petal of the red flower, riding my finger along the shock of white at the edge of it.

    When I was young, I thought I had seen God's love in a flower. I'd been walking home from a record store, cresting a hill into the city. A flower I couldn't name at the time, but came to know as a passion flower many years later, captured my attention. Its periwinkle tendrils swaying in the warm spring air, loose and free. It was short lived like most of my radical epiphanies, displaced by the day-to-day tragedies one collects through a life.

    With a hot sigh of tires on sand, an SUV filled with

drunken sorority girls parks next to me. Though they are laughing, one yells at the other for her reckless driving. The driver looks at me, whispers to the other and they laugh.

There is a smell in the air that I consider distinctly home. I'm unsure if it's pollen, or leaves, or grass, but it's a smell I only know here. In Seattle, I smell something different. Something salty and cold.

You drinking gin?

I turn to find my brother limping up the sidewalk. No, I say, soda water.

You're drinking gin, my brother says again, cracking a smile of stained teeth.

He sits down with me. Lights a cigarette. He adjusts his hat, fusses with his hair. Motherfucker, he says, it's a nice night.

The waitress comes and my brother orders three beers. It's a wise move I decide. There's no guarantee when she'll be back out.

I need to talk to you, man.

Okay.

I need to know where you're at with all this.

Meaning?

My brother looks away for a moment. He looks like he's wearing a mask of his own face. It's ill-fitting, the color off, a sickly sun-weathered tan dye with folds in places folds aren't meant to occur where the skin hangs loose but seems somehow inflexible. He takes a drag off his smoke. Blows it almost directly into my face and says, you knew this was coming. I just kept thinking it was all okay. You said it could happen and it fucking did.

I didn't know.

But, you tried to talk to me about it. I acted like a bitch. I'm sorry, man. And I'm sorry that I'm not helping you with Dad's place. I just, I just can't deal with that shit, man. It's just too much.

I want to tell my brother how unhappy I am with it. How much work I've put in. That it's hard on me too. But I don't. I don't say things like that. Not when people look like they're about to cry. Not when my big brother is tender. When he's not hustling.

Just be at the memorial service. It'll all be okay.

The waitress brings the drinks. My brother claps his hands together, rubs them as if to keep them warm, smiles. She waits for him to pay. He doesn't make eye contact with her. She looks at me. I pull money out of my pocket. Hand her a few folded bills.

Thanks, man. I got to wait 'till pay day.

I drink my soda water. Check my phone. In an hour, I'll be with Emma. In an hour, I'll tell her about this and we will lie on the bed and hold one another. I've never looked forward to seeing someone so much. My heart is unsteady inside me, part wanting to shrink, the other wanting to explode.

Dad always liked you best, my brother starts.

That's not true.

It's true. You're the only one who isn't fucked up. He pauses, swills a beer. I'm fucked, he says.

Two drunken college students come outside. As the door swings open, a school chant follows them. They stumble toward the curb. One slaps the other on the back. He says something about a girl. They erupt into laughter.

My brother, now finishing his second beer, says, how do you do it? How to do you manage to do everything right?

I don't.

Yeah you do. Look at you. You're at a bar having a soda water. Who does that shit?

I show my teeth in some way that's meant to be a smile and say, I have my own issues.

Bullshit. Look, I need to talk to you about the guns.

The guns?

The family guns.

I forgot about the guns. Forgot about the time my father took us shooting. About the time he accidentally fired a slug into the car when talking about gun safety. How he'd cried because he could have killed one of us.

There are no guns.

I know there are guns, my brother says, his voice growing edgy.

I'll check again, I say. The entire redirect has me off my game. I forgot what it was like with him. His thoughts always angling. If not for something tangible, for something emotional that I'd not anticipated showing. It's a skill he'd come by naturally through our mother, who always had some bridge to sell.

Can I just grab the keys from you?

I don't have them, I lie. The apartment manager lets me in each morning.

Shit. She can't stand me. Dad fucking told her I was addicted to drugs.

Are you?

Yeah. But, that's besides the point. Dad didn't have to put that out in the street, he says as he opens the third beer and drinks it. He drinks it in what seems like one swallow.

I look at my phone and say, I need to go.

So soon?

Yeah. Early morning, I lie.

We stand and my brother throws his arms around me. He slaps my back twice. He says, I love you, brother.

I love you too, I say.

As I walk away, I weigh the words. I don't know if it's a lie. I've been away for so long and my brother an addict for longer. My emotions have lost their compass and drifted so far from me, I begin to wonder if it's even possible to feel anything again, let alone this kind of sadness when my brother dies. I used to worry about getting the call that my father was dying. Now that it's finally happened, perhaps I'll worry about getting the call that my brother is dead. Sometimes I think it won't be long. I walk back slowly. I don't want my brother seeing where I'm staying. No surprises. No late-night appearances asking to sleep there.

I meander past the house and along the dark streets where the dogwood blooms radiate in the night, their fleshy petals lanterns in the gloom. A few fireflies linger. I watch their pulsing luminescence. I once stumbled upon a meadow in Indiana where the ground seemed electric. A dull shimmer on the grass as if the moon had spilled upon the earth. As I moved closer, head low and eyes wandering, I saw the thousands of tiny bodies. All of them burrowing. At the time, I thought they were all dying. A blanket of light fading away forever. I couldn't decide if it was beautiful or tragic that they were all dying at once. Then a familiar lack tremored in my stomach.

Is there a god, I say aloud as if speaking to the dogwood.

Now that my father has passed, I want to believe. I want to imagine my father in the land of no depression. I sigh. Walking away, I continue to wind through the streets. Looking into the windows of the homes. Most dark. Some filled with the haunting blue glow of a television. And what of the shows I watch? They've been forgotten. Replaced by hospitals, flights, layovers, layovers, layovers, and death.

I wish Emma was with me. Someone to speak in soft tones. The I'm sorries and I love yous. She's home. Working. Pulling words apart. Finding biological connections.

In the attic, I begin sifting through some of my father's things. There's a t-shirt that still smells like him. I pull it to my nose. Breathe deep. An urge to cry. I find a large re-sealable bag. Fold the shirt carefully. Slip it inside and seal it. Will it trap the smell forever? I don't know. Long enough, I guess. Some other time. At least once so I can smell him again.

There is a letter. I unfold it to find a crudely penned message I'd written my father when I was in high school. The penmanship is terrible and I'd drawn a cartoon replica of myself in the corner, something I did back then. *Dad*, it reads, *I know I'm not always the best son. I have trouble communicating. I'm hard headed. I guess this is my attempt at being better about this. I don't show you enough how much I care. These years have been hard on you and I know that your* [sic] *depressed. Today I found your journal. Pages after pages of "I love my family." I worry about you drinking. Maybe I drive you to it sometimes. I'm troublesome. I just want you to know that I love you and that I'm proud of you. I wish I could be a better son sometimes and maybe I'll evventaully* [sic] *be that. Love, Crag.*

My phone vibrates. The glow a pricker in my eye. Should I come over? Emma writes.

I set it down in my lap. Look at the boxes. Slips of paper. Notes. The warped attic floor and fat cat spread out and staring at me. I rub his belly. Roll the fur. Would it make sense to put her off? To have time alone? To consider the other elements of my life? My phone vibrates again. Unless you need space to process, she writes.

This is a sign.

Come, I type. My finger hovers. Then, I push. In the time before she arrives, I curl around the cat and look at the ceiling. To the spider building a web. I think of the inner workings of the arachnid. The gel of smashing it. How there are minute organs functioning to propel it. Then, I think of my father's organs burning. How the ashes they give the family will likely contain other ashes. Pieces of another family. I dream of ashes.

Of ashen people decaying in the wind. Of lovers colliding in a cloud. The world spinning and whirling and the bodies obscuring the sun in their own demise.

When Emma wakes me, I jump. The cat is gone. The room somehow gone dark. She kisses my mouth. Her lips cover it, undo me. I pull her atop me. My hands map her in the dull light. There is unfastening. There is tasting. There is sweating, moaning, releasing. When we kiss, I can feel her smiling. She tells me things. Secret things that are not about her family. Things about how I make her feel. She holds my head between her hands, her hair raining down around my face.

I fucking love you, Crag, she whispers.

I love you, Emma, I say. I want to say more but do not.

She rolls to the floor. The wood creaks. I put my hand on her thigh. Feel my cum on the inside of her leg. Coming from inside her. I offer to wipe it clean with my shirt.

No, she says, I like it.

This excites me. I am renewed. She is happy.

18

My father howled in pain whenever they moved him. Gritted his teeth when they shifted his bed. They attempted to help him with physical therapy. He bargained with them. Begged them to spare him. Just this once. Just this morning. Just this afternoon. Every day. They told me we had to get him to do it. I didn't know what to do. I wanted to trust the hospital staff but I wanted my father to be comfortable.

It was like this on the day I was dozing off watching horse races on the television. Emma's father had a winning horse. She and her family had walked into the infield to accept the award. It was a big deal. It was one of the biggest races in the world. If my father were cognizant, he would have been overcome with joy. He adored Emma. He lay there in some space between this world and that and I could only compare it to what I know. Floating, I thought. In warm water but always as if just waking in a new place, that sense of disorientation. And panic.

The physical therapist walked into the room. She had a nylon tension belt slung over her shoulder. It's time for his therapy, she said. I looked at my father as he slept in his bed. He can't right now, I said. She was young. Attractive. Part of me wondered if physical therapy was her back-up plan. If she'd planned to marry her high school sweetheart but it fell apart. She was a Kentucky beauty. The kind that didn't usually work. I don't want to come back, she said. And I don't want my father to be here, I said. Sometimes, I continued, we don't get what we want. She stared at me. I smiled. She smiled and said, okay, I'll come back at the end of my shift.

My father woke for a moment. He asked me something. I couldn't understand him. I stood up, the yellow gown hissing against my body. I want my momma, he said. I do too, I said and bent over to kiss his head, kissing my mask instead. I hated that. When he fell back to sleep, I walked to the nurses' station. Can we take him off the morphine and just do Percocet, I asked. I was worried that the drugs were keeping him foggy. I wanted to see if he was still aware. Still mentally strong. It had been weeks since his fall. There were few moments where he was semi-lucid. After his death, I would regret this decision. I would wonder if I'd made the wrong decision. If I had made the last days of his life painful for nothing.

At some point, the sun went down. Outside the world was buzzing and zipping and mating and burning. Inside there were only the sounds of the machines. When I eventually left to take a break, to feel the world as a living thing and not a dying body, I would have to wipe myself down in medical wipes. I would have to pull my computer out. Wipe it. My bag. My hands. My forehead. My shoes. I would have to cover everything in chemicals so that I wouldn't spread something. So that I wouldn't accidentally kill someone by infecting them indirectly. I no longer bathed in the bathroom sink in the hospital. It did no good. I wiped myself clean until I could shower and wash my clothes. I began wearing the same thing to visit my father. Wrapping the clothes in a bag so that Jim and Bonnie were safe. The skin around my fingernails began to crack. My psoriasis grew fiery. Painful.

I was hungry, but I didn't want to leave. I didn't want to stop watching my father's chest. I wanted to will his lungs full. Emma would write me. She would want to meet. She would want to tell me about her father's happiness. I began to think of her to pass the time. I closed my eyes for a moment. I thought of the contours of her body. The feel of her lips upon mine. I thought about her laugh and her touch. I wished my father was able to see us together the way he'd wanted. I wished that we could take him to dinner and laugh and they could make fun of me the way they had the year before when I'd just returned home from a trip to Germany. Make fun of my tight pants, my tailored shirts, my lazy eye. At the time, it had seemed like one in a series of forgettable moments, I'd not realized that it was tying she and me together in a way that would imprint upon me forever the meaning of loss and love and madness.

My father began to fuss with that flap of flesh that had once been a rotund stomach. He scratched and moaned. What is it, buddy, I asked. He didn't answer. I pulled back the white sheet, smelled his body. That strange mix of dried urine and mildew. I lifted his drop gut. His skin was on fire with rash. I placed my finger in the hot seam. He winced. I walked to his medicine bag. Removed his ointment and squeezed it onto my fingertips—the cream funny feeling on the glove. Rubbed it onto his yeast infection, he cooed a bit. That feels better, he said. So cool. I rubbed more in until all the hives were covered.

I walked out and told the nurses that they'd have to treat the infection when I wasn't there. The nurse nodded. Put it on the chart, I said. She nodded. Now, please, I said. She looked askance at me. I don't mean to be disrespectful. You're busy and it might get lost in the shuffle. She capitulated.

My father woke when I stepped back inside. He asked me to help him sit up. I searched the bed for a remote. I ran my fingers along the edges of the metal rails. I found pleasure in their coolness. How it penetrated the glove, the sweat, my skin. I found the button and pressed it. His body shifted. He surprised me by reaching his arm up. By grabbing the metal trapeze hanging above him. Fuck yes, I said in a moment of candor. He grunted. Shifted. Passed gas. Laughed. He scratched at his arm. He looked at the television. I told him about the race. Race, he asked. Race, I said. He looked at me. There was still a fog in his eyes. I'd hoped it would be gone. I'd hoped he'd look attentive. Instead, his eyes wandered, wide. I'm hungry, he said. What do you want, buddy, I asked. Fried chicken, he said. I took this as a good sign. Let me check, I said.

I asked the nurse if he could have fried chicken. She told me that they didn't know when the food would come but that chicken hadn't been on the menu. I ran to the elevator. I went to the cafeteria and bought some fried chicken and mashed potatoes. The grease was already seeping through the box, the oil wetting my skin. I could smell the dead meat. When I returned, he was asleep. The physical therapist was leaving the room. I tuckered him out, she said. This was a southern thing. To say tuckered or knackered. Okay, I said. Did he yell, I asked. Is he okay? He always yells, she said. He did well though. I could feel the chicken in my hand getting heavier. I set it down and put on my robe and gloves and mask and hat. I watched his chest rise and fall, the grease pooled on the food.

19

Emma stares at me. Her eyes wide, wet. My eyes always seem dry. Sometimes I think I hear them crinkle when I close my eyes. I think of eye gnats. Of their feeding on the eyes of cows and horses. How we smash them against our eyelids, their carcasses painfully removed with tissue. I touch her face, just right of her eye, where the hair fades into the skin. I kiss her forehead. Kiss it again. Pull back and smile.

You will come back, she asks.

I've been thinking about this, I say, and I think maybe I shouldn't.

Emma tilts her head, gives me a small growl.

Okay, okay, I'll come back, I say.

The sun crests the evergreens and a sash of warm light rests upon Emma's face. I'm transfixed by it, by her. The cut of her lips, the angle of her nose, the line of her bangs. She smiles and fine dimples manifest below her bottom lip. The things I've never noticed about her could fill a room. I touch her chin, my finger just feeling the indent before it vanishes. She takes my finger and kisses it softly. I lean my head against hers. We lock eyes, blurred by proximity.

You'll be the death of me, Emma.

Nonsense. Nothing beautiful can hurt us.

She pulls my bottom lip into her hers. Her teeth are against me and gone. I kiss her again, controlling it with a deliberate pause against my teeth. I place my hands on her hips. How long had it been since I dated a woman with hips? Had I ever? I can't remember. I've always dated emaciated women. Bodies like girls.

Bonnie's dog noses between us.

I look down and say, I suppose you want out?

The dog walks to the door. Emma laughs and holds on just a little longer than me. I feel her hands slip down my back as I pull away. The collie dashes outside after a squirrel, which makes it up the tree and turns to look back at the snarling dog. The squirrel twitches its tail. Makes small chirping noises. Emma walks behind me. Puts her chin on my shoulder. Her breath in my ear. Her hands slip around my waist. Leaning back, I say, fucking cute dogs ruin everything.

We should put him to sleep.

I agree.

We sway to the music of our blood. In the neighborhood, someone is trying to start a car. They grind at the ignition, but she never turns. I think of my father helping me with my car. The starter was going dull. Hit it like this, my father said, tapping the starter with a hammer. Once. Nothing. Twice. Nothing. Third time, it kicked in. Like they say, he said, the third time starts an old car. They don't say that, I said. My father smiled, they just did.

Where'd you go, Emma asks.

I was thinking of my father.

Her face softens. The corner of her eyes lower. I'm sorry, she says.

Me too.

As if prompted by some social courtesy she learned in her etiquette courses, she tells me I can talk to her about it. About anything, really, she adds. I think I know what she means. I get the hint, anyway. But there is no other thing, no other secret truth I'm hiding. At least not how I look at it. Just about the time I'm about to say so, the dog scratches at the door. The thunderous smack of its paw on the aluminum is alarming and shakes Emma and I from that disastrous track of conversation. I could kiss the mutt.

Where are the others?

At the vet.

Emma tilts her head, how long do we have before Bonnie gets back?

My blood shifts. Skin ignites. Breath deepens. Heart trembles. Does it matter. I ask.

I suppose not.

Emma takes the steps. I watch her calves. The give and take. At the top, I run my hand up her dress. She leans against me. I lift the garment over her. Kiss her back. She leads me to the bed. Pulls me atop her. Hands. Kisses. Breath. The world spins and spins and spins and spins.

20

Again they'd cleared my father to leave. He wasn't back to himself though. Still lost in a fog. I worried he'd never clear it. That his brain had drowned in toxins. That the pain medication had caused damage. That the fever had ruined him. Something. He reached in the air for the trapeze. He opened and closed his hand without speaking. I pushed the button on the rail of his bed. Eased him closer. He grabbed hold of the metal bar and lifted himself. This was progress I told myself. That a boy, I said. Something he said to me all the time. That a boy. Buddy. He rolled his shoulders some. Moaned at the pain. Eased back into the pillows.

I grabbed his breathing treatment device. Buddy, I said, we have to do your breathing treatments. Goddamn it, I'm not doing it, he said. I'm tired of you telling me what to do for Christ's sake. I nodded. I know, buddy. We have to do it. Fuck you, he said. He closed his eyes and whispered, let me sleep. There had been times where my father was upset with me in the past. Years ago, before I grew enough to know when I was being a prick. Admit when I was wrong. When we were young, we measured how angry he was by the space between *god* and *damn it*. Like measuring the distance of the storm through the space between the lightning and thunder. I stood with that device in my hands flipping it back and forth. I noticed, along the bony seam of plastic, the words *incentive spirometer* embossed. I set it down when my phone buzzed. Dad, I said, I have to go. It's the airport shuttle. He opened his eyes.

My father lifted his arms, I'm sorry, baby, he said. I'm sorry I was mean. He motioned his arms to me. Come. Come. I did. I leaned in. he grabbed me hard. Pulled me to him. Hugged tightly. I kissed his forehead. The mask still on. My lips hissing against the plastic and cotton. Still protecting myself. Always the coward. Scared of infection. My brother refused to wear the masks. Fuck that, he'd say. Fuck that, I'm not hiding my face from Dad. I should have pulled off my mask. That once. Just to kiss him.

I'll be back after I handle this stuff at work, I said. I'll be by your side during physical therapy. He said, I love you. I said, I love you too, Dad.

I walked away. My father waving. I left. Pulled the clothes from me. Tossed them. Got into the cab. Got into the plane. He will survive, I thought. He will.

21

Zelda is by my feet. I stare into the bathroom mirror. I can see her tail in the reflection. Its hair spreading along the side of the bathtub. Leaning in closer, I lose focus. My head against the mirror now. The chill of it, nice. Outside the rain pits and pats against the window. Pulling away from the reflection, focusing, first on the stain of my skin, then on the not-so-whites of my eyes. Upon my cheeks, I press downward. A hound dog. The lids of my eyes open and carmine. Puckering my lips, I release the hold and the skin creeps back. Slowly. There is no me in me, no him—only exhaustion. Just skin and bone and dusty blood that has all but quit me. Oh Dad, I say, I'm sorry for it all.

Zelda thrums her tail against the tub. The hollow sound of it resonating through the house, up along the walls and into the neighbor's flat, along the floors, and out the windows that are open in the front room, where it is lost in the hiss of cars. I should be running but my body won't rise to the occasion. I can only wander between this room and that, shuffling along the floorboards like a specter, then collapsing on the couch with closed eyes, only to rise again and twitch through the house with sighs and songs. Never finding sleep. Checking the phone when it vibrates but never picking up to face the questions I can't answer.

Zelda carries her bowl into the hall and feigns eating. I'm a terrible dad, I say, gathering her bowl to fill it with food.

There are moments I find myself on the fringe of sleep. My body becoming light enough to float. My legs seeming to lift from the ottoman. And then a jolt. A spasm. Something waking me. A large invisible hand. It's what happened to my father. I'd watch him in the hospital bed. Falling into the weightlessness of sleep when he'd shake and say something in the non-language of the morphine. Go to sleep, buddy, I'd say. I crash only when my body can no longer function. When I'm on the verge of being sick or my body feels riddled with ulcers. When I can no longer eat or hold a pen or speak a sentence without forgetting language.

The phone comes alive with Emma's number. She's in Los Angeles with her father. I let it go to voicemail. She calls again, and I answer.

How are you doing, she asks.

How can I answer this? I'm fine? I'm falling apart, and I don't remember how to function? I'm pacing from room to room and not eating and have waking dreams of pulling my teeth out with pliers? I say something else. Something along the lines of fine. Even as the words come out, I've lost them, and though I know this, I can't seem to stop it from happening. Emma laughs and I can't tell if it's kind or cruel and wonder if this is on me or her.

How is California, I say.

It's wonderful, she says. I went to the Museum of Jurassic Technology. I had tea and listened to a lecture.

I want to say great or cool or good job but say nothing and during that silence someone rings the doorbell.

Have a guest, she asks.

I guess, I say, sinking farther into the couch to hide. What are you doing tomorrow, I say.

Aren't you going to answer, she says.

I don't want to, I say because I know who it is, and even though I didn't invite her, Juliana is here.

Why not, Emma asks, her voice a minor key.

I don't know, Emma, because I'm trying to be alone.

Before Emma can reply, the bell rings again. Hold on, I say, and I answer the door and Juliana is standing there in the rain with a pizza and cake and tells me she didn't know which one would make me happier and Emma tells me to fuck off and hangs up.

22

Language, at least that is what it was meant to be. The click and hiss and oh. But it was sound. Nothing hitting the ear quite right. A mouth hitting the drum on an off rhythm. In the fold of the ear. Hairs and bones. Small, small, small. My skin tingled. Eyes swelled. The skin tightening. Wrinkles smoothing, perhaps. I forgot about the other person in the room. About the television. About the dog nuzzled into my armpit. My muscles contracted. Legs straightened. The light became unbearable. The weight of breath impossible.

The door squeaked and the floor moaned. There was still a voice. Still words that had forgotten how to be language. Sounds. Movement and small things shifting. I repeated these sounds. I nodded. Gave other nonverbals that were lost through the phone. Hung up. There was something prickling my skin. Hundreds of things. Grass. I was lying down. Staring at the sky. I couldn't remember lying down. I was watching TV. I was watching TV and the phone rang. Vibrated. Then, my back was against the ground.

Lights hit me. The neighbors' car as they rolled in from dinner. They spoke. A question. I replied, just looking. Looking at what, I wondered. Stars, I said to myself. Barely audible. Juliana's voice from the door. Another question. Stars, I said. Perhaps not an answer to her question. She sighed. She asked another. No. The door closed. She knelt next to me. Kissed me on his head. Left. Her car stereo: boom boom boom. And gone. I tried to remember my father's face. Project it. A new constellation. I knew this was coming. I'd spoken to the doctor. Forced him to speak to me directly. There was no feeling in me. A vast network of wet organs shifting. I was only aware of my body as a machine. My chest rising. Falling. Rising. When would it stop? The lungs in me that came from my father. The ghost of my father in every part of me. When would the world's machination suspend me? Cool my flesh? My breath? My eyes?

There was a gurney somewhere. A body draped in something like a sheet. A thing that was no longer my father. No longer human. Waste shaped like someone who I once knew. Once loved. A bug crawled in my ear. Its throng of legs tickled me. Circling the inside until there was a long screech almost quiet enough to miss. The dog scratched at the door. The stars remained still. Perhaps long since dead. The light a ghostly gravestone. The opposite of a body. A drunk walked by. He asked me a question. I said, fine. I stood. My knees popped. My head fogged. I tilted forward. About to keel over. A step and I was righted.

I entered the house. Pet the dog. Stared at the couch. It took me time to remember it. To remember the room. To remember my name and my skin and my life. The dog licked me. Her tongue warm and damp. I backed to the wall. Slipped to the floor. Pulled the dog between my knees. Buried my nose into her head. Kissed her and sighed. Stars, I whispered. We are not stars.

III

FIRE

23

Before the funeral, I went to a department store to buy my brother dress clothes. They hang before me in the family room of the funeral home. To my right an old man looks through food in the refrigerator. Is this yours, he asks. No, I reply. The old man then pulls out the food and says, it must be for everyone. I know better. Say nothing. Another family will come down expecting to find their wake preparations intact.

Emma sits next to me. She is amused by the old man stealing food. I stare at the clothes hanging in plastic. Curious if my brother will show. The guests are filling up the room above us. I can hear their feet. Their voices. The surviving friends of my father, distant relatives, my sister's friends. It's too much to go and talk to people. To go through the motions. Of handshakes and thank yous. The touching. Always the touching. I close my eyes. Imagine the ocean. The waves drumming a calm in me. The push and pull of the tide. The moon and the earth and the vast dark universe. This is where I go when the world becomes static and spark. To float among the waves, to float into the void. Emma takes my hand. She pulls it into her lap. Strokes my arm. Kisses my head.

My sister descends the stairs into the family room. Her boyfriend's daughter in tow. Why is it in the basement, the girl asks. I don't know, my sister replies. I introduce them to

Emma. There is conversation. Condolences. Remarks as to how pretty Emma is. How lucky I am. Yes, yes. The teenage girl becomes shy. She looks at me. Smiles. She twists her hair. Emma takes my hand into hers. I release it and walk to the vending machine to look at the sodas. I stand there, unable to process the words. I push a button to hear it click and then walk upstairs to get water.

My uncle stands at the top of the steps. He looks to me. Smiles, his ears impossibly big. I nod. I pass him and take a long drink from the fountain—cold water clearing my throat, parting me in some way. Momentary pleasure. My uncle stalks me, his steps moaning against the floor. I don't want to turn around. What would happen if I just kept my face down, finger depressing the button? How long would my uncle wait? I stand upright. Turn around. Accept the old man's hand. Shake.

Your old man was one hell of a guy, he says.

Thank you.

He'll be missed, he says as his free hand picks his nose. Always picking his nose. I'd forgotten about his habit and now the already awful handshake is unbearable. I attempt to slide my hand away, but my uncle won't let go.

I'm sorry for your loss.

Someone comes up the stairs, a labored breather. Before I can turn around, I know it's my sister.

Why are you here, she asks.

Without letting go of my hand, my uncle answers, I want to give my condolences.

For what, she asks, you did your best to make him feel small.

Now, it's not the time to air this out.

Pulling my hand free, I turn to my sister and say, we need to handle the paper work. Will you come with me? I turn back toward my uncle and say, thank you for stopping by. My father would've appreciated it.

You're a good man, he says. He pats me on the arm. Walks away.

Why are you nice to that dick?

Let's just get through all of this.

You know what he said about dad after mom died. What he said about you. About all of us.

And it doesn't matter. Higher ground and all.

She looks at me and gives an artificial smile. Like this, she asks.

Just like that.

Where's this paper work?

There isn't any, I say.

Goddamn if you're not the smart little bastard, she says.

Emma emerges from the stairwell and it seems as if the world is born anew. My shoulders feel lighter. Tolerance of the world recharged. Her smile is practiced and flawless and from a place of comfort I'll likely never know. She sidles next to me. Slips her fingers between mine. She asks if I have my eulogy. I pat my chest. The paper crinkles in my interior pocket. She kisses me. This is her world. The world of people doing human things. Of thank you notes, wedding presents, baptisms, and eulogies. It all fills my throat, chokes me.

It will be brilliant, she says.

I thank her but don't believe it will be. There is nothing brilliant left in the world. The sun somehow has grown duller. That stars have started to vanish. She kisses my cheek. By the ear. I laugh, partially at my penchant for the melodramatic and partially because it's true. Her kisses are brilliant. Yes, there is that.

My brother has managed to enter and dress without notice. He walks around greeting people in the new clothing.

A peach shirt, tan kakis. A stained white ball cap. Dingy white leather sports shoes. He charms the guests. Smiling. Laughing. Working them all for something without them knowing it. Some of the people I know, some I remember with a prompt. Others I can't place. There are far more people here than we expected. People filling the seats, standing along the walls, lingering in the anteroom. The funeral director brings in more chairs. More people file in. They come and shake my hand. Hug me. Their touches make me want to shed my skin. They tell me of the good my father did. What a tough football player he was. How brilliant. How funny. None of this helps and I wish I could tell them this much. Thank you, but it doesn't fucking help, so leave me alone.

Years before, a girlfriend told me that the same thing happened at her father's funeral. How it upset her. They didn't know. They didn't understand that her father slipped into her room after her mother fell to sleep. Began sleeping with her. Touching her. That he'd gotten her pregnant and took her to have an abortion. How it didn't stop until she left the house. Took a train to the coast. Lived in a commune and loved a woman. That she'd only come to the funeral to make sure that he was dead and sealed in a box and buried. That he might stop stalking her in her dreams. She might not expect him when the wind awoke her in the middle of the night. Will I find some other side of my father—some horrible secret released now that he is gone? I know I won't.

Two strangers approach me after the service. They introduce themselves. I recognize their names. I've seen their notes to my father, scrawled in shitty cursive on an airport cocktail napkin, their promises to him forever unfulfilled. As they talk to me, I begin to recognize their voices, ghosts drifting through a country club landscape, where there are fireworks and peacocks strutting around a pool. How close our families had been before it all went to shit. I want to tell them what it was like in that room with my father. I want to tell them that I'd read their notes. That I'd seen their replies when my father asked they honor the agreement. To share with them the debts of my father, but I say nothing. Thank them for coming. Walk away with my stomach hurting. The way it does when I am about to fight. That awful adrenaline. They know what they've done. Staring at a photo of my father at the end of his life wasn't going to make them feel better.

When it is finally over, the room emptied, chairs folded, boxes of the paterfamilias distributed, Emma and I leave. We run through the terrible rainstorm. The thunder and lighting. The wind. We join the others for dinner. My brother sits across from me. He talks to me. What a beautiful ceremony. How cool it was to see their father's football buddies. How nice the flowers. He scratches at his neck and arms and legs. He taps and pats and sniffs. No, he won't be eating. He has things to do.

Emma pulls me toward her, whispers, he's not so bad.

I rub her leg, kiss the crescent shaped wrinkle next to her ear, and talk with my brother. I ask him about the job he doesn't have. The job he lost but insists he has. I indulge him while the others eat stale bread, undercooked meats, scalded pastas, and wilting salads. My brother was right not to order.

Not long into the meal, my brother leaves. It's still raining outside. Cats and dogs as they say. I offer him a ride. My brother declines. Later, when I go to the bathroom, I see him outside buying crack with the money people gave him at the funeral. He will smoke the crack and think the world is coming after him. He will fly and soar and panic and panic. Louisville is a good place for addicts. A place they can live in flop houses next to families, next to young couples planning to have kids, next to council women, because no one asks about anyone's business. It's a town long raised on looking the other way until it's too late. I grew up with addicts. Accepted them as commonplace, drinkers, smokers, pill poppers, junkies, and gamblers. For most of my life, I was the outlier, the writer who didn't drink. The writer who didn't get high and make things worse. No, I always made things worse well on my own, stone sober.

※

It really was beautiful, Emma says as we lie down to sleep.

I place my hand on her naked hip. Become aroused. Kiss her. I love you, I say, more than I can possibly tell you.

I love you too, Crag. I love you more than I've ever loved anything.

This is the moment where I usually vanish. Become a third person and see the fallacy of sex and love. Hover over top. My body paralyzed with embarrassment. But with Emma, I don't. I lose the outer edges of myself, they slip into her flesh. Our bodies a landscape. We moan and gasp and bite and suck. There is nothing in the world beside this and when it's done, we spoon in the sweat and cum and sigh. I fall to sleep in her arms and wake hours later to Bonnie calling up the steps. Sorry, she says, sorry for all the noise.

What noise, I say.

A drill sounds and she says, that noise.

Emma swings her feet over the bed and I follow. Some of my clothes are on the floor. Folded in strange patterns. Some are torn. They have labels on them. Words in Latin.

Oh my god, Emma says.

It's okay, I say.

No it's not, she says.

Of course it is, you didn't even wake me, I joke.

She pulls the clothes into her hands. She looks at me, her eyes wide. I've destroyed them, she says. Her hands shake as she pulls things together, almost as if she's gathering the evidence to destroy. As if the removal of the evidence will absolve her from the deed and she can go about her day free of this thing that seems to haunt her. And if she were to kill me in her sleep, would she dispose of me in the same manner? I laugh without quite understanding why.

Are you laughing at me?

No, absolutely not, I say, scrambling. Without a plan, I begin a story, when I was a kid, I used to wet the bed. It was something to do with anxiety. I was in a school that didn't work for me and all that stress fucked with me. My mom tried everything she could to help, from having me repeat, I will not wet my bed, twenty times before sleep, to prohibiting liquids after five, but nothing worked. One day I was invited to a sleep over and I asked my father if I could go. Mom was gone, I don't know where, so my dad let me go. As you can guess, I pissed my sleeping bag. I woke early, cold and wet. Before anyone noticed, I rinsed it off in the bathroom, changed, and walked home with my things.

A drill hits a brick and the floor vibrates a little. Emma stares at me so I continue, no one knew and eventually we figured out what was stressing me out and things got better. Look I say, removing the clothes from her and tossing them to the side, this shit happens. Don't add more stress by worrying over it.

She shakes her head for a moment, but her bangs remain straight above her eyes. I slide next to her and place my hand on her hips—the skin there soft and tight. She lies down and I kiss her hips, her navel, make love to her anew. We laugh in hushed breaths. Be careful. Don't get caught.

✸

After we eat at a Chinese restaurant, Emma excuses herself from the table to brush her teeth. Always brushing her teeth. How proper the lady. What a good child. I stare at the fish in the aquarium next to our table. The striped cichlids, the green terror, the yellow and blue. And, as if it is meant to be, or they were placed to remind me, I recall a dream from the previous night. I place a finger on the tank and the green terror follows, wagging her tail, puffing her gills.

What is it, Emma asks when she returns.

She's laid eggs. She will kill the other fish in the tank.

How do you know?

I had fish for a long time. Green terrors are beautiful but territorial. Whoever designed this tank probably didn't account for that.

Is that what you were thinking about, Emma asks, some sparkle in her eye like she knows something.

I had a dream last night.

She twirls a straw and says, tell me about your dreams, in a terrible Swiss accent.

It's an anxiety dream.

Aren't we a couple of nervous Persians, she says then she holds the straw out like a microphone and says, what happens in your anxiety dreams? Do you show up to teach the wrong class? Naked?

Nothing so typical, I'm afraid. In my dreams, I forget that I own an aquarium until I happen upon it. The water is dirty. The fish starving. I feel horrible. Negligent. I feed them. That's usually it. I wake up. But last night, as I was shaking food into the tank, I realized that it wasn't food but anti-depressants. I put my hand in to remove the pills but I'm too late. The fish are too fast and eat the white pills.

Why fish?

When I was a freshman in high school, we sold our house because my father had lost his job. I had an aquarium and was going to give it to my sister. She was supposed to come and get it on the day I packed my room. I put all the fish in separate glasses and set them in the closet. I left her a note as to where they were.

And she never came…Emma adds.

She never came. I think about those fish sometimes. In those tiny prisons. Suffocating in the dark, I lift a finger and the green terror follows it. We underestimate the fish, I say, that's why people don't care about killing them. But inside those little bodies are complex systems pumping blood and generating thoughts. Maybe it's not metacognition or higher order thinking, but…

But it's a life.

A life. It's worth something.

Emma places her hand on my chin. She pulls me to her. Goddamn it, Crag, I love you.

24

The day after my father passed, I met with the Dean. I was sixes. I was sevens. Seattle was pissing rain. The hard tap of it against the building. I'd been inside for well over an hour and still felt wet. She opened a folder. I'm sorry to have to bring you in for this, she said. But rules are rules, she said. I nodded and looked at the corner of the folder. I looked at my name written in blue pen. The tab slightly bent. Dean Temple stared over the top of her glasses. She looked at the pages in the folder. She looked at me. She looked again at the pages. She took in a breath. She told me that a student saved my emails. She said that the mother and the girl brought them into her office. A formal complaint. Skipped the department chair altogether. You did miss *a lot* of class, Dean Temple told me. The words lost definition. I focused on her mouth. The corners tucked into dimples. The fine wrinkles along the top and bottom. A smoker. Years of suck and release. A fluorescent bulb tremored above us for a brief moment. Yes, I did, I managed.

A dramatic pause. A fingering of papers. She told me the student dropped the charges. That the student was satisfied with her final grade. I knew complaints might come. I felt it was best to pad the grades because I'd missed so much. When I had been in that hospital room the last few weeks. I did what I could remotely. Emails. Phone calls. Video chats. Half human. My mind in some other realm of living, but students, they always wanted more. When I'd drop one grade, they wanted two; when I'd meet with one, they'd want to meet again, for me to tell them how to write, how to structure. More and more. Meet with me for a tea. Write a letter. Dance, dance, dance. As if I didn't have a hundred students. As if I sat on my ass all day waiting to help them.

My stomach felt wrung from the inside. My breath hot and swelling in the neck. I crossed my ankles, knees out, and it occurred to me I got this from my father. The way he sat to give his stomach room that drove me crazy as a kid. I pinched my stomach beneath the table. The Dean pulled several pages from the file. Slid them before me. I lifted my fingers. Accepted them. Sweat stowing away in my fingerprints. Before I could flip the paper over, the Dean said, we can go about our lives now. I stared at the contract for the following year. My eyes burning along the lids. She stopped as if struck by a thought and said, I'm sorry, I forgot to ask, how is your father? I told her that he'd passed. She offered condolences. They sounded odd there. In that room. Like props.

I can't shake the phrasing from my head. Go on with our lives. Did I have a life to go back to? Would my life ever be the same? I had already begun seeing my father in everything. In elderly people who used to irk me in lines. Chewing on uncooked mushrooms in restaurants. Sitting alone with their walking canes. Hands shaking.

I pushed the pages away from me. I heard words coming out

of my mouth. They were measured but I was on fire inside. I steadied the shake in my hand as not to show my emotions. I won't be returning, I said.

The Dean's eyes widened. Her mouth worked a muscle. She was worried that it was because of the incident. Rules are rules. Etc. Etc. No, I lied, I need to be around loved ones. I wondered whom I meant? Emma? I thought of Zelda. Of going home and collapsing onto the bed and pulling the dog into my arms. Thought of the time the neighbor shot my dog when I was a boy. How I ran to my father and we took him to the vet and saved his life. The worry in my father's eyes. More for me than the dog. And then it all vanished and I was back in the room. Away from my father's eyes. Away from my youth. The bikes and games and dogs.

Because, she said, if that is the reason, I can assure you have our full support. It's not, I said. This is not what I wanted to say. I wanted to say that it very much was the reason. I wanted to say that the formality pulled me away from my father's side. That I was not there in the moment my father most needed me. The moment where he pulled back the veil of the dead and the living and slipped through. When his chest sank and stopped rising. That I was on a couch, two thousand miles away when my father died in an empty room.

Instead, I shook her hand. Told her that it was my pleasure. That I was glad we could talk. My body was that academic machine. A device of reciting and balancing. It took over when my heart was burned up. Still, I might have wanted to consider it. To think it through. To weigh the options, but did not. Could not.

This was unlike me. I had been so calculated in everything I'd done in my life. Resisting alcohol, drugs, temptations, always overachieving because I feared the poverty I'd experienced as a teen. Always career first, over family, friends, and love. And there I was crushed under the weight of death unable to think clearly. It would be months before I'd realize that my emotions had hijacked my reason. That despite my ability to remain polite, I made a bad decision. Realize that I simply gave in and let my body guide me. Guide me out of the office, into my car, and back into my bed, where I looked at the ceiling and wished that something, anything, would expel from me these stones of regret that weighed so heavily inside me that I could scarcely pull a breath from the air.

25

There is a last-minute job interview after the funeral. I go to Boston. Parts of my father are in a green plastic box. I wonder which parts. I hope his heart. His brain. Emma helps me pick out a suit and drives me to the airport.

    Why are you doing this if you're planning to move home?
    I don't have a job lined up here.
    Emma is thinking. I can tell because she's biting her lip. I know how much you love your work, she says.
    I do.
    I guess Boston isn't so bad, she says.
    Not so bad, I say.
    She kisses me goodbye, her mouth hugs my bottom lip. She wishes me luck. There is sunlight in her voice. It warms me. It stays with me on the flight. I like this. A lingering kiss. How many lips had I touched without this? She is worried that I'll get the job. I worry about it too. It might be the end of us. Certainly, it will end sometime. Eventually. It's the way of relationships. People don't stay unmarried this long in life unless they're broken. Unless they're good at endings.
    I arrive to find a van waiting. It takes me to the campus, where I meet the department chair and faculty—then the students and Dean. Students. The Dean. I teach a class. Hand out activities.
    They do an Oulipian exercises to begin. The Dean likes

this. He is excited. Child-like. He and I prefer the same type of soda. He likes this. Says so. He solves the problems I give them. He asks how the exercise functions as a tool. I explain exactitude. Precision. Constraint. Finding possibility in limits. He points to my bag. To the green box.

    Is that another exercise? he wonders.
    No, I say, that's my father.
    They laugh.
    No really, he asks.
    No, really, I say.
    I won't get the job.

※

It's a long time before Emma speaks to me. I stare at her face as cars and trees and houses blur by along the Watterson Expressway. My impulse is to push. To pry. To open and see the insides. I don't. I don't say a thing. I let her chew words in silence. Her eyes occasionally wander my way, but she doesn't turn her head. She feels my eyes on her. When she speaks, the words are angles and glass.

    If you're meant to live in Kentucky with me, why do the interview?
    I won't get the job.
    Not the point.
    But I won't.
    If you do?
    I say nothing. Look at the car in front of us. Its bumper stickers crooked and sun-faded. *Not my President! No Blood for Oil! Arms are for Hugging!*
    Just the fact that you'd entertain the idea, she says.
    I'm blindsided by this. I begin speaking before I think.

Stumble through *oh-babys* and *it's-not-like-thats*. Defensive, but I've already lost. Every word comes back upon me, the edges sharpened by her silence. My pulse electric and syncopated. When she looks at me, it's not her. It's someone else, I'm quite sure. Someone else's eyes pushing out of her. My skin is all scattering bugs. It's difficult to hold my shape.

She says, I'll drop you by to get your dad's stuff, but I'm not staying. I'm going home. I'm tired.

I'm not sure how to argue, to ask her to stay. I agree. It's best, I think, she's not herself. And when we do arrive, I step out of the car and say a loving goodbye. She smiles and gives me the finger. It might be playful. I choose to laugh. Close the door and she leaves.

There's a rickety shopping cart the seniors use to help them with things. Its wheel flips, hisses, stutters. The front wheel catches in the small space between the door and cab. My ribs smash into the handle. With the wind gone out of me, I lift and push and grumble and make it inside just before the door closes. It's a slow rise. As if the aged can't take the momentum. Cautious in every place. The door opens, and I wheel the cart, more mindfully. My father's door is unlocked, the life tab no longer flipped to red.

I place a mirror, plates, photo albums, this and that into the cage. Roll it backward. The china vibrates in its box. That thin sound of gilded edges ready to chip. I keep my eye on it as I return to the ground floor, where I'm greeted by a congress of elderly people. They surround me and begin touching the cart. They are slow, but in a group problematic. I can't zig. Can't zag. Their knuckles rosy and swollen. Fingers, thin and veiny, ghost the objects. Romerian zombies growing around me, slow but steady.

One woman says, your father had promised me the mirror.
Another says the china.

He left me no written instructions, I say.

There was a nice chair he had, a man begins.

That was spoken for, I say.

He had a television, a woman says.

I really must be going, I say, trying to lean into the cart in a way that might signify intention to leave no matter the consequence and the hint is not lost on them. They, one by one, turn away. Shuffle back to their places. Chairs, couches, corners. It takes some time, some rattle and shake, but I get the thing to my car. Put my father's stuff into the back. Looking over to the building, his window with the lights off until the living turn them back on, something in me closes, some internal eye gone to sleep.

I drive to my new apartment. Things still boxed. I unlock the door, Zelda on the other side losing her mind. Yips and barks and hops and jumps. I rest my head against the wood before twisting the knob.

26

I had a crush on a German model that I'd seen in some music magazine when I was in high school. She was lovely. Supple in the places a young man desires. Her lips full and pouty. I bought the magazine. The photo of her made my body shake. It was like nothing I'd ever felt before. I cut the photo out. Taped it on my wall. Soon I found another. I taped that to the inside of my writing binder. The book I carried everywhere. She was with me always.

The others would catch on. See her beauty too. America would sign her to deals. Post her on the sides of buses and buildings. She was on television. Stumbling through interviews trying to mind her v's and w's. She did a mall tour that came to Louisville. I was in college then. I looked my age. Baggy clothes, an unfortunate goatee. Long stringy hair. My friends coaxed me out. To the mall to see the scene there. Moms dressing their daughters up to be discovered. Makeup and hairspray. Starved in miniskirts. If you bought a bottle of perfume, you could wait in line and have a free calendar signed. It seemed foolish to me. To wait so long. To spend money just to speak with her.

I could see her on her throne. Small in the distance. By then she'd lost her child-like looks. Thinned out. She looked older than me, though we were the same age. Her blouse likely more expensive than every piece of clothing I owned. Still, just seeing her at that distance, made me nervous. I asked an attendant how long the wait was. She said three hours and fifteen minutes. People started showing up at five in the morning she told me. Soon the spectacle of it wore off. We left.

When I came home, I found a box on my bed. Inside it was a signed calendar and a bottle of expensive perfume. I sat on the edge of my mattress and opened the calendar. A photo of her on the beach in a bathing suit. On a horse, her hair flaming behind her. In Paris. On the month of my birth, she wrote: *To Crag, your daddy loves you, you little prick.*

Sometimes I think about my father waking at five. Standing in line at that mall. Teen girls and their mothers all around him. Chattering. How his feet must have ached. I'm not even sure how he knew who she was. Knew I'd coveted her. I think of how I lost the calendar somewhere along the way years later. I wonder what she must have thought when he asked her to sign it that way. What had I done for him at that age? Complained about things he cooked. Moaned when he asked me to clean out the basement stairwell because it was all spidery. Argued with him over nothing all the time.

How does one atone for being a shithead for the first twenty years of his life? Had I atoned? Part of me knew that my father and I had transcended into a friendship that was unlike so many others, but another part of me fussed over the details, brought back to life the corpses of old conflicts.

27

Light on another building. Bricks and mortar and windows and bums sleeping. Emma is on the bed with me. There is nothing else. The dogs sleep together in the corner. One wakes, raises an eye to me. I wave, and the dog puts her head back down. Sighs. There is no direct sunlight. Shadows upon shadows. A bum says something to the other. Something about a tarp he'd found. Emma looks to wake but does not. Her hair loops against her face.

I ease off the mattress. Walk to the bathroom. I poke at the black circles beneath my eyes. Pull the skin. Squint. Where is he? Where is my father? It seems the further time spans forward, the less I see of my father. Sometimes I catch the old man's ghost. In the corner of my eye. I lean in. Press my head against the mirror. Lean more until the glass creaks.

One of the dogs walks down the hall. The clicking of nails. It's Zelda. She noses in. Whines. Food. I can't feed her. They will fight. They will snip and snap. The pit bull will crush her. Tear her. It's not fighting bred into her. It's dogs. She's sweet. But still a dog. I take a bowl, pour food in it. I hear Chelsea stand. I slip the bowl in the bathroom and shut the door when Zelda enters. I pour a second bowl and slide it in front of Chelsea. Emma rouses.

Are you feeding Chelsea?
Yes.

She doesn't eat this early.

Sorry.

Can you stop her, Emma begins, her voice sleepy. Then, never mind.

I step into the bathroom. Pet Zelda while she eats, while she wags her tail and huffs food down nearly choking herself because she knows the other dog is close. It's okay, I say, Chelsea won't come in here.

Emma curses in the bedroom. Fuck, she says, what the fuck?

I feel it in me. Some slivery thing. Sliding around my bones. I say nothing. Wait for it. A knock comes at the door. I'm using the bathroom, I lie.

Your *dogsitter* sent you a message. Emma raises her voice. Makes it nasal.

Okay, I say.

Okay, she asks.

Not okay, I say. Intonated like a question.

Not okay, she confirms.

I bend over Zelda's ear. Whisper, *Jesus, what now*? Kiss the dog and leave. Let the door open. The dog conflict avoided. The human conflict to ensue. Taking the phone in my hand, I read the message. I miss your touch.

Emma is shoving things into her overnight bag. She doesn't look at me.

I look back at the message. It's two hours old. I don't ask why she picked up the phone. Why she read my messages. I can't find words. Something collects in my throat. Paralysis.

Well, she asks, are you going to say something?

There's nothing going on.

Tell me the truth, she says, this is your chance. You can tell me the truth right now.

I had a thing with her. It was brief.

Recently?

Months ago. Before all of this.
How did you meet her?
Why does that matter?
You withheld this from me. I want to know why.

There's no reason, I tell her, because the only reason I can think of is fear and that won't sit well with her. I know this.

We met at a reading.
Your reading?
Yes.

Oh great, a *fan*, she says, the word exaggerated as if it's simply an impossibility, as if she thinks I'm a fraud. The edges of my ears grow hot, my nose feels like it's expanding as blood rushes to my face.

How long did it last? Did you like her?

I tell her. I don't know my own words. They are foreign to me. Not the truth. But once they're out, I can't say that they aren't true. I'm just saying things because I really want to tell her to go fuck herself for her condescension. I stay the course but don't want to. Soon, I can't even hear the words coming from my mouth. They come without catalogue. Why would it matter anyway. She'll leave or she won't. She has no reason to be upset. This is not an upsetting thing. It's before her. Emma slings her bag over her shoulder. She's crying. It seems too quick. The tears. I can't react. I say nothing. Don't move.

I need to think about this.
I nod.
I'll call you later. She says, then stutters, I don't know. Maybe. Maybe I'll call you later.

She calls the dog, but the name she calls is not Chelsea. She says, mys, and pats her thigh. Chelsea comes to her. Emma puts her collar on.

I watch her walk out. Her hair moves in waves along her back. Her calves engage and release. The door closes behind her. It does not slam. Zelda looks at me. She comes to me. Sniffs my hand. Easing to my knees, I look into her eyes. What the fuck, I say. Zelda licks me. I fall onto the mattress. Zelda hops onto the bed. We spoon. Sleep.

※

The city all angles. As small as a stone. Old and new. They've flattened some of the older buildings for a stadium. It's strange down here. The days are filled with ties and sunglasses and suits and southern drawls. This business or that. The night is filled with blowing bags, homeless people, and a wind that seems to come from nowhere. Despite their best intentions they can't seem to revitalize downtown. Perhaps the stadium will change that. I sit in a sandwich shop overlooking Main. There's no reason to be downtown. I'm an interloper. A man behind me talks long and loud. This deal or that. It's some repetition of things said before. I work the dough in my mouth. Overpriced peanut butter. I wanted to go somewhere completely different from my barren apartment. Some place where the world buzzed. When I was young and poor, I would fold a few dollars, pack a book, and come down here to play pretend, to imagine I wasn't poor and wasn't struggling. I'd see the men and women with their laptops, so rare at the time, so expensive, working through lunch. I wanted so desperately to be a success. Maybe I thought this would center me. Remind me of some purpose I'd forgotten. I can't say. I just came. I fold my receipt. I do so without great intention. A crane. Some lingering habit from my days in college. Leaving them for people. Anything outside of the ordinary. Until it becomes ordinary.

I wonder if I would've felt the same affinity for this part

of town had my father worked here. His offices were always in some cluster of office buildings out among the suburbs, back when the white flight was pushing away from the city. Sometimes it was in another city, another state. Unlike most fathers, he didn't move my family with him. He didn't relegate us to the prefab homes that so often appeared in the fields, as if summoned from the dirt. Golhomes, he'd called them. Clever word play, I once thought. No, he never moved us away from the arts district. The Highlands. Music and art and teens begging for change. I never considered my father cool. He was anything but. Listened to tin pan alley. Drank shit beer. Watched *Hee Haw*. Watched *Lawrence Welk*. Yet, he knew his children. Knew where to raise us so we weren't programmed. Passive. I, however, had a job here in this world of glass buildings. Once. After college. Writing this or that for an advertising firm. Two, three, ten things at once. I packed my lunches. Rode my bike along the river, through the rain and cold, heat and night. Until I tired of writing for mega churches, liquor companies, fast food corporations, and tobacco vendors. Before I moved to California. To Seattle. Just to return. After it all. No savings. Everything blown. There is no triumph in Kentucky. Only dogs with tails tucked.

    My phone vibrates. A message. *Hi! How are you? I love you.*

    I stare at it. Look outside. Swallow. *Everything is okay*, I write. *Zelda misses Chelsea.*

    Should I come back, she responds.

    I will come there. You shouldn't make the commute twice.

    !

    !!

    !!!

    I want to ask if she's over it. I want to know the ground. Stamp upon it. Test it. Do not. I know better. Know her as powder. Fixed to blow. The sandwich between my fingers is unbearable. The grape jelly through the bread. Bloody gauze. Tacky to touch. It slides from my hand. Clumps on the butcher's paper. I fold it. Retie the string.

When I arrive at Emma's, she is in her study. There are pieces of fruit: pineapple, orange, star fruit, kiwi. All of the skins peeled away. The seeds, skin, and pulp all arranged in piles. Each labeled with notes written beneath. A Mitchell BNCR is mounted to a stand. The lens aimed at the piles. I lean in to read the labels, but Emma stops me.

It's not ready, she says.

Sorry, I say, I can't understand what you've written, anyway.

Good.

Emma cleans her scalpels. Begins putting away her pencils and index cards. She drops a card and bends to pick it up. I look at the samples again. She has written in reverse, but also in a variety of languages. Some words I've seen and can place the origin but not the definition. It's like watching a French movie. I have heard some of the words before but don't know their meaning. If anything, it distracts me. This is when Emma catches me again and asks me to walk Chelsea while she cleans the room.

28

My brother wanted a BB gun. He spoke about it with my father. Began obsessing over it at dinner. Sometimes, he'd leave comic books out, splayed carefully next to my father's keys so the colorful ad on the back was close enough for my father to notice it. *Be an expert marksman! Fight the Indians! Hunt!* At the time these seemed like real things to us. My brother and I, obsessed with *The Rifleman*, with *The Lone Ranger*. We would play Cowboys and Indians in the yard. I, being the youngest, was always the Indian.

One day, when complaining to my father that my brother always made me the Indian, my father sat next to me. Son, he said, you're part Cherokee. I looked at him. Our people, he said, are strong and proud. I laughed at him, my skin nearly transparent. Look doesn't define you, my father said. This was lost on me. Years later I realized that everyone around Louisville claimed to be part Cherokee, and like many of them, my family was not Cherokee. Standing up, my father patted me on the back and took me to the back yard. Stood me by a tree. Called my brother down to join me. We walked to his car and he opened the trunk. Removed a box from Sears. Opened it and pulled out a BB gun. Reached in his pocket and pulled out a canister of golden metal pellets. Fingered them into the gun. Wait for me, he said, leaving the gun in the grass. When he returned, he had a hammer and a nail. He pulled a target from the box. Nailed it to the tree.

We stood twenty feet away. My father pumped the rifle. The more you pump, he told us, the harder it shoots. He pumped until he could pump no more. My brother grasped at the gun. Gimme. Gimme. Gimme. All fingers and teeth. No, my father said, the Cherokee were here first. Stepping behind me, he slipped the gun into my hands. Showed me how to cradle it beneath my arm. How to aim with the tip. Moved it around some as to better my aim. Shoot, he told me. Leaves twirling to the ground on the unseasonably warm autumn day. My hands wetting. My brother chiding me. Hurry. Hurry. Hurry, he said. I squeezed the trigger. Not hard enough at first. Harder. A *paw!* from the gun. Before I'd lowered it, the BB stung me on the throat. I fell. A pause. My hand to the neck. And. Tears. My brother laughed. Laughed and laughed. My father, quick to his knees. His beer belly, a shining moonstone beneath the sun. Goddamn it, Son, he said. I'm so sorry, he said. I should have known better. He helped me up. Walked me to the kitchen. Got me ice. Got me an ice crème sandwich. Went to the pantry. Returned to the yard with a piece of Styrofoam. Put it under the target. I stood in the kitchen and watched my brother, the natural athlete, hit a bull's-eye with his first shot. Never again did I pick the gun up. Occasionally my brother would shoot me with it. He played with it every day. Saving allowance to buy more BBs.

One Saturday, shortly after we got the gun, my brother yelled for me. I was watching cartoons. My father next to me talking business on the phone. Drinking a beer. Laughing. Saying, son-of-a-bitch. Saying, damn. This was our Saturday usually. He'd go to the market before sunrise, bring home donuts and cold milk, and wake us to watch cartoons while he drank beer. I grabbed my third glazed chocolate donut and ran outside. Look at it, my brother said, pointing to a squirrel high upon a wire. Its tail twitching as it eyed us. My brother leveled his piece. Fired. The squirrel fell to the ground. A soft thud. He ran to it. Said, I wished I'd killed it with one shot. I watched the creature. On the ground. Its front paw grasping quietly. Its lungs quick. Its eyelids jittery. I don't know why I did it, but I called for my father. My brother punched me. Fag, he said. My father came out. Looked at the tiny animal. Grabbed the gun from my brother. Walked into the house. Came back with a bag and a brick. Are we going to take him to the vet, I asked. My father told me to look away. I did. I heard the brick hammer the skull. It was enough to turn me all liquid. On the ground. I can't remember him taking my brother inside. Can't remember what he said. I only remember after. When we were eating lunch. When he said that sometimes the kindest act a man can do is to put a thing down.

These words play in a loop some nights as I think of my father on the bed, fading. Was I making things worse by cheering him on? Should I have stepped back and let him join his mother on the other side of the veil? It cut me two ways, the right of it and the wrong of it.

29

Maybe I need some room. To deal with this my way. A few months apart. I could use the time to work, Emma says.

I look to my hands. Some nervous habit. They are pale, the right stronger than the left but both weaker than perhaps they should be. Stammering, I say, I just moved here. It's not easy to just walk away.

I think it'll be best.

Is it really what you need?

Emma looks at me and grabs my hands. Oh, Crag, I love you more than the world. I just don't know what else to do.

It seems to me that couples work through things together.

We push the subject between us. Zelda seeming to see it. Her eyes moving with it. Or with our bodies as we animate to speak. I agree. It fills me. A lake of sadness brimming at the edge of my throat. My heart seeming to slow and speed at the same time. An unsteady trot. I watch her leave my apartment. Her calves catching the dim lamp light like some dust at the edge of the universe. Golden and falling just out of eyesight.

✸

Zelda noses into me. Rests her muzzle upon my thigh. I walk her. In the burgeoning fall that is not as cool as the northwest, but cool nonetheless. The first leaves of autumn crush beneath my feet. It's too quiet. I'd grown so used to living in a bigger city. A cat crosses the road. A rounder. Zelda comes to attention. Stands still for a moment. Majestic the way they get. Sniffs. Lunges. I give her some leeway but not enough. She stops at the length. The pressure harness pushing lightly at the meat between her ears. She eases. Looks back. I take a knee. She comes to me. Licks my face. Wags her tail.

I'm hell bent on nothing, I say. Zelda whines and licks me again. Like a movie. You know, I say, you watch me needle at it until there's nothing left. I pet her head. Lead her to Cherokee Park. We walk the trails. The moon is nearly round. Heavy in the air. Setting or rising. I forget which. I walk to the hill where children swing by the pavillion. Release Zelda from her leash. She bounds away. Chases something up or around a tree. The metal is cold on my fingers. Smells of rust. The chains moan with my movements. I attempt to recall the first time I used a swing. Cannot. Can only recall other times I sat on these swings. Sometimes with women. Sometimes after. After they'd left me, or I'd pushed them away. I wave my hands. Rattle my fingers. Pop my neck. Ease my legs. Release my breath.

If I could molt, it might feel better. Shed my skin. Shed something. This is something I always think. Since first learning about snakes or spiders. It must be refreshing. I bend back. Crack my spine. Fluid this way and that. Clearing between the bone. Zelda returns. She has a stick. Her tail, a wild fan. I take it. She nips and yips, frantic. I throw it. She retrieves. We do this down the hillside. Through the trails when possible. When we reach the road, I hook the leash to her. We walk home. The air is still. Almost solid. The room smells of Seattle. I miss it there. It's funny to me how things carry smells. Smells like memories. The dog goes to her bowl.

Drinks water. Lop. Lop. Lop. Until she gags. Then. Lop. Lop. I feed her. Release her harness. Drag it to my bed. Lie down and find sleep easily.

※

I awake. The sky bright. From what I can tell. Perhaps overcast. I check my phone. There is nothing. No message. No email. Nothing. I write a message. Backspace. Write again. Backspace. Shut the phone off. Drop it on the pillow. Listen to men outside. To the news of the alley. The forecast as told by the men who take residence between my building and the next. Rain. Most certainly rain.

My stomach is empty, but there is no space in it for food. Something awful has taken residence. Something heavy. It moves and moans. Somehow the world has become unfamiliar. The sun a different sun. Emma a different woman. My skin no longer mine. A borrowed fragment from my father. My mother nearly erased from me. It's not long before the rain comes down. The pitter pat of it upon the air conditioner. The men outside let loose their tarps. Rattle them straight. Drag them atop their heads. I roll to my side, body tucked, fetus shape. Sigh. As the breath leaves me. Something else fills my lungs. Anti-air. A vacuum. I message Emma. Stare at the phone. See myself in the tempered glass. My hair a fiery whip. I look my age. As if it came upon me over the night.

The rain begins to hammer. The wind kicks. A sumac moans beneath the howl. In the corner of my eye, I spy a blue tarp flying past my window. One of the men outside shouts. The other laughs. The phone vibrates.

I have lost my way in language.

I read her message twice. Three times. Another. I move

the words in my head. Roll them on my tongue. Breathe them in and out. Spit them. Suck them. Weigh them for subtext. There is nothing I can make of them. I write as much. Emma replies instantly. It's a photo of a stack of labels. There is a knife. Pieces of fruit, vegetable, a plant, all cut apart. I call her. She doesn't answer. I think to leave a message, but only inhale and disconnect. Putting on my running clothes, I look at the dog and shake my head, not you, girl. I step into the rain. It's heavy and hot. Unlike the rain I've grown accustomed to. The rain that refreshes. Cools to the touch. Without stretching, I splash onto the sidewalk. Scarcely ten minutes and the city is already streaming. Leaves and litter swirling.

In the woods of the park, my passage sways trees. The branches heavy with water become trumpeting cataracts. The rainwater colliding with that which comes from above. The thicket bites at me, first in nips and then in long tears. The blood washes into my socks. The pain is comforting. A memory of being human. I push harder. Raise my knees. Bound on my feet. Do what I'm not to do. A pinch in my ribs. An invisible hand crushing something soft inside. Push. With each meter, my breaths become smaller. Until I stop. Until I must lie down. Until the ache is so present that I know hurt. The rain pools around me. Rises against me. I roll to my back. Let the water pound my eyelids. Then, I walk home. Passing the Daniel Boone statue that the tornado of '74 allegedly spared, I look at the stately Victorian homes, their livingroom and bedroom lights visible because of the cloud-gloom. I'm reminded of my mother making me alphabet soup and grilled cheese on a rainy day, but can't shake the idea that it was really a commercial I saw as a child and that my mother never did such a thing. Had my mother's addiction poisoned all my memories? Have I softened my father's bad days because of his good? Circulating these concerns, I make my way through the streets until I'm standing at the entrance of my building a while before opening the door.

Emma is in my foyer. She looks at my legs. Heavy and damp, my shirt stretched around my neck. She hugs me. Cries. Neither of us speaks. We enter the apartment. She pulls my shirt from me. It falls to the floor with a clomp. She pulls my shorts down. Kisses my thighs. My pelvis. We make love on the floor. The small of my back sucking and hissing at the hardwood.

30

Shortly after my mother died, I returned to the room to find my father on the edge of her bed cradling her, limp and folded, between his arms. I watched from the doorframe. He wept. Rocked back and forth. My breath was too loud, so I held it. I held it until my throat burned. Until the veins in my eyes crept into vision. Until I nearly blacked out. But my sister came, her sniffle ripping the moment from its hinges. Our father turned, easing my mother out upon the bed. Smoothing her limbs. Her gown. Her tubing. A square of sunlight on her distended belly. Her jaundiced skin, withered to what was left of her. Our father kissed my mother's forehead. Patted it as if to make it stay.

After we attended my mother's wake, I asked my father if my mother was his one true love. No, he said, I loved your mother, but she was never my one true love. I thought I saw it in his jaw. A stone buried there. The gum and meat and tooth arcing around it. So, I pried. I dug. I massaged. Came at it from every angle. To see it. To show him the truth he was too proud to accept. What a shiny rock, I would say after unearthing it. See how it bends your reflection in the smooth surface? See the layers that time left. We can count them to find the exact day you fell in love. But it never came from him. On some nights, after my father had passed, after he was cremated, I would stare at the box of ashes and wonder if the stone was in there. Floating in a sea of powder. Scented like burning chocolate and cow's blood.

It's something I'd return to. Again and again, but I never got an answer that satisfied me. I don't believe he did. It wasn't his thing. The poet or the lover. He was a thinker. A problem solver. His love was for his children, never choosing one over the other. It didn't matter the trouble we caused. The good we did. Maybe at the time it didn't seem romantic. The way I wanted it. Yeats and comets and forevers. But it was, perhaps, the most romantic. The purest love. When I had interviewed him on camera last summer, I asked it about him again. He fidgeted at first. Rolled a cane between his hands and stared out the window. I said, I've turned it off. He began answering my questions. When finished, I told him that I'd lied and showed him the footage. His face lit up. It looks old, he said. Like film we shot of your sister when she was a baby. It's an app, I told him. I explained how it worked. He watched and made comments here and there. I made cucumber sandwiches. Cut them diagonally. Set them on his chipped plates. Poured lemonade into mason jars. Brought the meal to the table. When I took the phone back, slipped it into my pocket, he said he'd like to do it again. The next day. And so we did. Every day for two weeks, I came over and interviewed him. Made us sandwiches. Watched him nod off in his chair after eating.

I began editing them. Cutting and pasting. Adding music. Fades. I began telling narratives of his life between the sections. Histories he'd not told. Histories involving the family or his college years or fights he'd been in. The interview provided me with the opportunity to know my father in a new way. Through a direct line and not the filter of my interpretation. But still, I found ways of understanding him that I'd not anticipated. He liked, for example, talking about his work; his eyes sparkled and grew wider around the edges when he spoke of his innovations, his deals, his struggles.

This happened when he spoke of his mother too, so I asked him again. Was mom the love of your life? No, he said, no hesitation in his voice. Unless you mean by way of friendship. I asked if he'd dated other women. If you're asking if I fucked other women, women after your mother, then yes, but I never dated any of them. I didn't want to expose you to the kinds of women I met at bars.

When he was on the cusp of saying something negative about someone, he always couched it with something positive. He did not like to speak ill of people. Not even when he spoke of those who'd betrayed him.

I worked on the film for months. It was to be a Father's Day gift the following year. I would load the documentary on the digital tablet he wanted and gift them both to him. But he'd not make it to that day. The film would later die on a hard drive during a lightning storm.

31

The mirror needs to be cleaned. Water marks, streaks, dust. I stare beyond them. Into an artificial depth. Squint. Pucker. Smile. It's no use. Even in the dim light of window. Nothing. I close my eyes. Let my feet feel my way to the tub. Sit on the edge. I breathe into my hands. Cup them harder against my face. I think of a prayer I said when I was a boy. When the wind rattled ghosts from trees. Scattered them between the cracks in the house. Witches and devils creeping. Always creeping. Then, I stopped. In college, I tried again. Looked for God. Searched books. Temples. People's faces. Despite my disbelief. Habit and superstition. A collection of thoughts. I began to recite a nightly meditation. What's the harm? That stopped the day my father died. The compulsion to believe was too strong. To think my father was in some Hollywood heaven. Lawrence Welk conducting an orchestra in all white. My teeth begin digging into my bottom lip. The small ridges, born of stress grinding, puncture me. There is a hint of blood. I ease off. Lick at the tiny scrapes. Fight the urge to let go. To fall back into the tub. Letting my head rattle against the wall or soap cove or faucet.

There is a light tapping sound. I don't recognize it as a knock at first. It sounds as if the pipe is working something through. Then again. I go to the door. Emma is in the hall. Her eyes are raccooned. Her hair a nest. She's in jeans and a shirt with *Kentuckimaniac* printed in white script.

That's some shirt.

Emma throws a letter at me. Says, that's some letter.

I bend to pick it up. Emma walks into the living room. Does a circle around the coffee table. I begin to flip the letter over and Emma says, it's from Juliana.

Oh, I say, setting it on the bookshelf. I walk into the kitchen. My hands shake. My stomach aches. I pour a glass of water. Shut the door. Think better and pour another. Emma is on the couch. She's opened the letter. She throws it on the ground.

Fuck you, she says.

What?

Fuck you.

Emma, what's it say?

It says, you're a fucking liar.

I set the waters on the table. Collect the card from the floor. I attempt to read it. The delicate handwriting. My mind won't absorb language. My breath's growing smaller and shorter. I close it. Stare at the letter pressed figure of a sailor looking to a star. Open it again. See words.

Miss you.
Empty.
City.
Nothing.
Wish.
Could.
Move.

My finger hovers over the small heart at the bottom next to her initials.

A heart, Emma says. So sweet. *The town's not the same.* Fuck her. She can have you back.

Emma is always quick to escalate, but it's been so drastic lately. Fear, a crack in the ice and me in the center, looking to find my best exit—I attempt to choose my words carefully. There's nothing here. I'm not lying, I say. As the words leave my mouth, her face goes all shadow and I know the ground is shifting and I'll be all wet soon.

This is just like the last time, she says.

It's not, I say.

Nothing in my head connects. I'm turned around. Don't know what's the truth anymore. Every motive, move, word under her microscope. Even the truth feels like a lie to me. So I speak. Speak and fill the room with words. They come from me and I'm not even listening anymore. I'm thinking about how weak my knees are. How thin my flesh. Thinking of ways I can leave. Jump through the window. Run through the door. Toss the bookshelf over and escape. Words. Words. Words. It's just impulse. Response. Like when I was a boy. When my brother threw punches at me. My body collapsing. My arms and legs flailing without intention. Wild in panic.

Emma shakes her hair. She stands. Sits. Stands. Turns in a circle. She walks to me. She looks to want to kiss me. Her face is hot. There are tears. She raises a hand to her cheek. Palms it. Lowers her hand. Backs away. She walks to the door. Opens it. Turns around. Slams it behind her. You're, she begins. She stops. Looks in the air as if something is coming to her. A feather. A leaf. A something I can't see. Sketch, she says. Then she mumbles something in her secret language.

So many words I don't know. Are they insults?

I try to level my voice, hold the shake of panic still. I think you're acting out. There's nothing here. I point to the card. I shake it for effect. It's what they do in movies. I don't feel these things the way she does. That rush of lava spewing out. I freeze. I engage in performative acts. To look like people.

Nothing, I say.

Fuck you.

She opens the door. Walks out. Leaves it open. Her shoes drum the carpet. The security door opens. Closes. Then nothing. I think to follow. Think to call. To be people. But I am not. I do nothing. Choose to accept this as the point of changing things. The door closes with a creak. The brass knob cold. I lean against the wood. Feel my breath against it.

Zelda comes into the room. Her head low. As if in trouble.

Where were you? You never miss the chance to see Emma. I pull Zelda's head between my hands. Bury my nose in the scruff of her.

Zelda walks to the couch. Sniffs. Whines. Comes back, her tail lifeless. She licks my hand. My face. I lead her to the kitchen. Dig in the small pantry for a treat. Tell her to sit. To play dead. To roll over. To shake. Give her the treat.

✺

Most of the day passes. The sky muddy with clouds. I run errands. Here. There. Take Zelda for a run. Work to reorganize the closet as best I can. Remember my first apartment. How I'd no closet. Just a rusty shelf where I'd stack my clothes. Did it have a fluorescent light in the bathroom? My bathroom in the damp basement of my father's rental home had one. Some mornings I'd walk along that basement floor, through streams of water on rainy days, across the strange bugs that often crawled up from the sewer drain. I'd click the fluorescent light on to prepare for school. To shower in the rusting shower, taking care not to let the mildew laden curtain stick to my skin. At night, the bulbs made me sad. I don't know why florescent lights make me sad. Perhaps they reminded me of some time past.

The mid-century home my grandmother lived in. The ghostly colors cold and lonely.

Everything is swirling in me. My past, my father, the move home, unemployment, my small, dark apartment, the argument. There are no more boundaries. No abjection. No I or ego or superego, just one mess of everything at once. A dial between every channel at once, every frequency prickling. At least Emma is tangible. At least she makes me feel something. Some connection to the world that seems to have vanished beneath me.

I don't know what to do. I pace around the apartment. Between the bedroom and the living room. I move things around. I hang a painting. I drink a glass of water. I clean the bathroom. I come back to the closet. I begin re-organizing it. Unpacking boxes. Collapsing them. I open a box filled with shirts. Nested in the center are my father's remains. I stare at the green box. My lip, a thin crescent swung tightly upon my teeth, is dry. I lick it. Pull it into my mouth. Bite. Then I set the box on a low hanging shelf. Next to a crate filled with folders.

How are you doing, I ask. I'm sorry you're still in a box.

The box does not answer. The box never answers.

I'll get you to the ocean one day. I touch the box. Think to hug it. I don't hug it. The nametag is fragile. The ridges of it crinkle beneath my fingertip.

Upstairs the neighbor begins having sex. There's loud music. There are a series of noises. Slow squeaking and then faster. The man moans, followed by silence. Someone hops down from the bed or couch or chair and walks to the bathroom. I think of my cum on Emma's leg. How much she likes it. Does she like it with other men? The idea hurts me in a way I'm not expecting.

I take my father's ashes out of the closet. Place them atop the bookshelf. Say, you were the one who loved her so much.

The box doesn't respond.

Zelda makes sleeping noises on the couch. Her paws twitch. She's chasing something. Something's chasing her. She's never known fear before. How can she dream of something chasing her? There's a boom of thunder. The neighbor's date yells.

Damn, she says.

Zelda looks at me.

Damn, I say.

She rests her head between her paws. Sighs. Closes her eyes. I pace again. Not returning to the closet to finish my chore. I'm too exhausted. Or too restless. Or can't be bothered. I'm out of touch with myself. Can't get my thoughts together. I say things like, I want my life back. I wish I was dead. I miss you. Where the fuck did I go wrong?

I grow dizzy from pacing, I crawl to the floor. I lay with my back half on and half off the oriental rug I'd bought at a Swedish furniture store. I watch the fan. Turn to my side. Wish to cry. Wish to sleep. Do neither. My muscles feel thin. My skin loose upon me. I'm certain my hair is falling out. My teeth cracking into their foundations. My gums turning to gel. Whoever I was six months ago found a way out. I'm now just a body moving along. It's rotting. Eventually someone will smell me. Bury me. Set fire to me. Gather my ashes and stuff me in a box. My sister will store me with all the other bodies she has in boxes. Perhaps she'll sit us around the table at Thanksgiving. Serve us all portions. Pray. Drink and laugh and share stories with us. And when she dies, what?

32

I'd always wanted a proper leather jacket. A motorcycle jacket. Plain and classic. Nothing over the top. A waist buckle. Button shoulder straps. They weren't cheap. A few hundred dollars. My first leather was a third-generation jacket already spray-painted, thinworn from years of use. It wasn't what I wanted, just what I could buy with the money I'd cobbled together doing odd jobs. There's not a lot of money for a thirteen-year-old kid to make. I bought it in May. Wore it every day. Through the brutal Kentucky summer. Through autumn and into winter. Until I was at a metal show, dancing in the pit. Run and run until someone falls. We all fall. Get up. Begin again. That night someone came in with a straight razor. There was blood. When I made it out, my skin was untouched. My jacket, not so lucky. I bought two hundred safety pins and mended every cut. Frankenstein's jacket. It was okay. It was punk. It worked.

This was not lost on my father. He watched me in the living room pricking my fingers on pins. Mending the cuts. How'd that happen, son, he asked. I assured him it was a skating accident. That I'd fallen on an embankment. That the thin leather just fell apart. He asked if I needed help. I said that I did not. He drank his beer and watched football. He watched me put the jacket on every morning, walk out the door, head to school. Around

Christmas the following year, I was sitting with my mother at her apartment. She'd been drinking. Her voice soft, her speech filled with S's. How people's voices get when they're in that way. Your father is going to surprise you for Christmas. He got you a leather jacket, she said.

My mother always ruined my father's surprises.

I looked through all the closets that night. Found the jacket hidden among his suits. It was all wrong. Futuristic. The sleeves ribbed, the back tapered into a V. It broke my heart. To be so grateful at the gesture but to know I'd never want to wear it. I called my mother. I asked her to come over one day and look at it. To tell my father that she knew it wasn't right and suggest they go back and trade it in. He'd never know I'd seen it. Never know she gave him up. A perfect crime.

Christmas came. That morning, I wandered upstairs. We gathered around the television. My dad and I. We ate fried Spam. Drank Pepsi. He handed me a bag. The smell of new leather breaching the paper. I was nervous. Scared to open it. Prepared myself to act happy. Prepared to wear that horrible jacket because I loved him. I parted the edges, slipped the coat into my lap. Unfolded it. Smiled. He'd swapped it. It was right. As teenage boys are wont to do, I played it cool. Awesome, I said. This is awesome. Thanks Dad.

He sniffed. Took a drink of his Diet Pepsi. Sorry your mother ruined the surprise, he said. My heart sank. Sorry, I ruined it, I said. He assured me that I hadn't. That it was best I got what I wanted. But I knew that he wanted to surprise me. To get it right.

Not two years later, I went vegan. I couldn't bear the idea of wearing leather, so I sold it to a friend for next to nothing. At the time, it was just another thing my father had given me, but as I grew older, more prone to introspection, reflection, or just sentimentality, I started to regret selling it. As things went in those days, friends came and went through my life and so it was I didn't keep in touch with the woman I'd sold the jacket to. But tech companies had different plans for us. They began connecting us through social media algorithms. On the day I received a request from a near-stranger-once-friend, I inquired about the jacket. Assuming she too had parted with it. But she hadn't. She mailed it to me at no cost. Some days I'd pull it out of the closet and wear it around. I'd think of that day my father gifted it to me, of the frustration in his voice when I told him I'd sold it. Maybe I'd not righted the wrong, but it felt nice to have it back, like I'd pulled some piece of him back from the void.

IV

RESURRECTION

33

The waves push and pull in their cycle. The sound of it calming. It's the heartbeat of this new world. Crawling with lizards and spiders, sprinkled with sand and sun. On those days when tropical storms roll in from the horizon, I watch it from the shore. Allow it to wash over me, winds kicking sand here and there. The palms behind me whipped and hissing.

I hear the ocean when I lie in my cot. Allow it to set my pace while I wait tables, cook, bus tables, clean the pool. It has become my timepiece. The sun wakes me. Nightfall reminds me to sleep. And between are the waves. But there is no work today. I sit, watching the sea, with my back against the bole of a palm tree. The occasional vessel punctuates the horizon in a slow crawl. A feral dog, a shaggy thing, wanders, sniffing for anything the sea may have kicked up. He wanders several meters south before doubling back. He sees me, comes to me, hesitant, his tail tucked but waging. The tourists feed them. Sometimes adopt them and try to smuggle them in. Zelda growls and the stray heels.

No tengo nada para usted, I say.

The mutt whines. Zelda, grown lazier by the tropical heat, stands. Bares her teeth. The scruffy dog retreats. Looks back as it gallops. Returns to water to find rotting fish.

They're harmless, I say to Zelda.

She sniffs me and licks my ear.

Someone approaches behind me. The sand crunching beneath their bare feet.

Señor ¿no trabaja usted hoy?

It's a boy from the neighboring village. I don't know his name. I call him Poco. I feed him when I'm working. Steal away to the back door and hand him a plate. I don't know for certain, but I suspect it's the only the meal he eats. I don't ask because part of me doesn't want to know. I've given up worry.

No, Poco, hoy medito al lado del mar.

¿A que sí?

Sí.

He sits next to Zelda, pets her. She rolls to her side. Allows him to stroke her undercarriage. Sand pipers scurry about on the fringe of water. Running back and forth with the surge of it. Poco sighs and looks out to the sea. Emulating my meditation. He often seeks me out when he doesn't find me working around the hostel. Knows he'll find me here or in my room. He'll sit outside my window and sing, a la vibora, vibora de la mar, to himself, drawing stick people in the sand. I'll rouse and feed him and he'll take me into town or into the hills. Teach me Spanish words for plants and animals. We don't speak much but I enjoy his company. I don't know if he's an orphan or if he goes into one of the small adobes clustered along the streets of the town. His siblings sleeping next to him on the floor. A tapestry of limbs. I guess not though. The kids around here run in packs. Brothers and sisters. Once I asked Poco about a hairline scar that runs along the side his face, from the corner of his right eye to the edge of his jawbone. Mal hombre, he said. Nothing more. Some nights when I stare at the shadows on my ceilings, I wonder about Poco. Like some of the strays, will he disappear one day? Lost in this landscape that bucks and hisses?

We are far enough from any areas of Mexico that are unsafe for tourists, yet, we aren't so far removed, like those high-end resorts that college kids visit, that it's unthinkable one of us could be kidnapped or killed. Especially since most of us are stumbling our way through the language. A simple miscommunication could go a long way out here.

Devon's hostel caters to people who skew away from places like Cabo for their winter vacations. People who want some semblance of authenticity, save for the discomfort of confronting their privilege in the face of poverty or the threat of their baggage getting knicked—hipster vegan artist types. Most of us who work here know Devon from Seattle. We're all escaping from something. Most don't talk about it. Don't discuss our reasons for being here. It's the one thing we don't get into. For our work we get food, shelter, and a very small stipend. Everything is cash. At night most of the staff gather on the beach and drink around a bonfire. The guests occasionally gathering around. I hear them from my room. Laughing and singing. I keep to myself mostly. Write longhand by lamplight. My sentences shorter and shorter because of hand cramping.

Poco is spooning Zelda. They're sleeping. I think of Emma. Spooning Chelsea before life went completely sideways. Think of the nights I stared in the mirror to see my father inside my own reflection. How strange it all seems now. On this beach. A world away. I'm not sure I've looked at myself in the mirror in weeks. I wonder if there are mirrors where Emma is. How she looks at herself. Does she see her mother there?

A couple wander onto the shore from the hostel. He's wearing a pair of cutoff jeans and a rock shirt with a font I can't read. She's wearing a bikini. Thin. Black. The woman rolls out a blanket, lies down. The man looks to me. Raises his hand. I nod. Kicking off his slip-on shoes, he chases sand pipers to the amusement of his partner. Poco rouses to the laughter. Looks to me. I shake my head.

Gringos, I say.

He laughs. It's an upward scale. Chimes. It gives me a tremor in my heart. Pleases me in a way I'm not familiar with. Despite his weathering, Poco is still a child. He takes the straw hat from my head. Places it on his own. It covers his eyes at first. He tilts it back. If I had a child, I think I'd want him to be like Poco. Resourceful and grateful for things that come his way.

Vamos a comer, I say.

Poco nods with great enthusiasm.

We walk along the shore until we arrive at a path where the sand has been smoothed by vacationers. Between the mounds laden with bracken. We walk into the outside bar, where Anne is cleaning glasses and singing along to the stereo. I recognize the song. It's the Carter family. Something seems to shift in me. I imagine a shark. In utero. One looking for its sibling to eat. Sleek and wet.

Two whiskeys, Anne says, winking at Poco.

I pull out a stool, help the boy onto it. Adjust the hat for him.

We'll take some waters. I say, then looking at the smile on the kid's face, say, fuck it. Two Cokes. We'll have Cokes today.

When I return with plates of beans, rice, and tortillas, Poco is halfway through his cola. Anne has taken my hat. It looks nice on her. The way an oversized dress shirt looks on a naked woman. Sometimes we flirt. It never goes further. There's nothing in me to share. Anne pops the lid off my Coke. A fine mist rises from the mouth. It's been months since I've had one. I sip it and it reminds me of home. Of magnolia blooms, trimmed grass, the smell of tar sticky along the cracks of summer asphalt.

You okay, Anne asks.

Fine, I say.

I sit down, slide the plates over. Anne touches my arm. Traces the edge with her finger for a moment. Stops at the elbow.

She looks at Poco. Says, debería haber visto Crag cuando llegó aquí. Pálido como la luna.

Poco, mouth filled with rice, laughs and says, hombre luna.

I slide my Coke over to him. Eat.

34

In Kentucky, I'd heard the news from someone else. They wouldn't let me see her. They said that I was the cause. A cause. It was all unthinkable. There was a mistake and eventually I believed the truth would out. But it was already out. It would take me six months before I'd accept that. I did what I could. I walked around the park. I ran. I ran and let the sweat collect in my shirt. I ran until my legs grew weak. Until I fell into the forested world around the path. Until I thought I'd die. My lungs failing to rise. I wept there. The thought of the dog walking to her with trust and love. The scalpel running over the fur, the wild stare of betrayal on Chelsea's face as she bled out. Then the parsed pieces, labeled and jewel-like beneath the lights.

The mosquitos stung me. Their proboscises long withdrawn before my slaps. I thought of what I could have said that set Emma off. She'd grown more suspect of me with each text I received from Juliana. It came to a head when I picked up the dog. The note she found that I'd not seen. The tender heart etched onto rice paper. What love letter, I'd asked. I thought I could have been a better boyfriend. Emma began questioning me about the particulars of the affair. I began to recall them as best I could. How we'd met. How it began. How it had ended. I'd framed it as an affair. To cushion it, I suppose. It was a romance.

It had been beautiful at some point. But I didn't know how to make it work. I built in a door. A way out. There was always an exit with romances—except with Emma. Maybe it was too short lived, the turbulence too exquisite, but I never wanted to leave her. When we were apart, I felt a faint ache somewhere in the back of my chest and when we split, I was driven to such distraction, that I couldn't manage my duties.

My memory had been flawed. Things I should have remembered were lost in a fog. I had been forgetting my phone. My keys. The names of close friends. The facts were coming out in spurts. Sketchy, she'd called me. A liar. I'd lied about a couple things. Yes. A liar I wasn't. The facts had been falling in and out. Some still fall in and out. Interference happening inside me. I had begun taking mushroom supplements. Eating spoonfuls of coconut oil. Nothing was helping me. Was this what it meant to age? To suddenly forget how to recall?

I had told Emma what I could. I'd tried to put it to bed. To be forgiven for something I shouldn't have needed to be forgiven for. A relationship before her. It would not be put to bed. She would wake it. Walk it around. Throw the sheets on and off it. Flick the lights. Shout and cry. Each time she asked new questions that prompted new answers. Forcing me to remember. Memory is not a linear narrative, I had said once. Fuck you, it is, she had argued. It had better be when I ask you to be honest.

A jogger ran by me. She slowed down. Jogged in place. Are you okay, she asked. I waved to her. She ran off. I heard children playing in the distance. At the swings on the hill. In the part of the park where middle-aged men didn't collapse into the trees. Where bodies were never found torn to pieces by rats and raccoons and all manner of things. I knew I would have to leave. That I would walk back to my apartment. That I would remember Emma kissing me. Making love on the unmade mattress in the living room. Too eager to fuck to finish moving it into the bedroom. The dogs playing with a bone on a rainy Tuesday. Emma saying things in her secret language as she watched. I felt a pain in me I'd never known. A new empathy. Chelsea, I said. Then, goddamn.

Once, my father had told me that we fall in love with women's children and pets. He'd told me not to fall in love with them. Not to feel the compulsion to adopt and shelter. But surrender was in his voice. He knew we were powerless to such things. We would always fall in love with the world around women.

It was a snake that displaced me. I heard it and then felt is slither along my arm. I jumped up. Scared it away in the move. It was a harmless garter snake. I began the walk back. It seemed so much farther as if the way grew longer with each step I took. The paths and roads stretching out before me like they do in bad movies when the camera is focusing on the damsel in distress. I arrived to find Jim on the porch. The pug curled in his arms, snorted and wiggled. He said he was sorry. He said that he hated her for it. I told him to keep it a secret. To forgive her. It wasn't her fault. It's not your fault, he said. I nodded. Everything horrible in the world felt like my fault then. My shirt was heavy with sweat. I pulled it off. I threw it against my wall. It stuck for a few seconds. Slid down. Thanks for coming by, I said. He followed me inside. I sat on the couch. I watched the dogs play. I wept. I wanted not to. But I couldn't help it. Jim put a hand on my shoulder. There there.

35

The moon is full. My room glowing. I watch the sheet in my window ghost back and forth, twisting at the hem. I recall my father waking me to watch a lunar eclipse as a boy. How gentle his tap upon my shoulder. We sat on the back porch and watched it blush in shadow. I wanted to share this with my own son one day. When I was in college, I thought I'd marry and have kids. That I'd teach and come home to a family. I'd wear sports coats, jeans, dress shoes. I'd carry a vintage briefcase. I kept meticulous journals, saved toys, protected personal awards. I'd show them to my children. Look what I did. You can do anything. All those in some landfill now. I have nothing to pass on and no one to pass it on to. Middle aged. If that. I've slipped to the wrong side of forty. The dark side. Where the body falls apart. Heartburn and headaches and sleeping wrong. My only tether to the world a dog, a street kid, and a group of people I barely know. Everything else left behind. My siblings likely wonder where I've gone. Perhaps my sister more than my brother. My friends. I left notes. Vague explanations. Promised to reach out when I'd settled. When I'd found peace. Only Devon knows. The secret is safe.

    I walk outside, wander past the couples drinking by the pool. Slip into the community supply room. Grab a flashlight, a knife, canteen. I drive through the empty streets of the town. Up into hills.

Zelda and I hike the trails. Into the trees. Where the spiders creep. My face occasionally catching their webs. I remember the time we went up north. To a man-made island. Rafts made land by roots and vines. One with a forest of baby dolls. I was told by a local that a small girl haunted the island and I shouldn't stay overnight. Once she told me that, it's all I wanted to do. I couldn't find anyone to take me. I rented a hotel in Mexico City. Left Zelda in the room. Called Anne and told her what I was doing. Said, if you don't hear from me tomorrow night, come get Zelda. The city is dangerous, she said. You'll come get her, I asked.

Yes.

I rented a canoe and paddled out to the Isla de las Muñecas. Camped under the rusty moon. There was a moment where I thought I heard a little girl crying. I tilted my head. Held my breath. Tried to still my heart. All to listen closer. And if she did manifest? If she did call me to the water to drown myself, would I have gone? It's only now that I know I was hoping for it. Hoping for anything to happen that was out of my control. Walking the streets at night. Going to dangerous bars. Hiking into parts of the country known for cartel murders. At the time, I'd convinced myself I was discovering life by walking in the face of danger. But danger never found me. That trip seems like a lifetime ago. Veins of the previous year still pumping poison into me. Me pulling away but their elasticity dragging me home. There was scarcely a day I didn't think of returning those first few months. Instead, I tried to push my boundaries further, out past what I had known, what I had imagined. I began to see the beauty in the world. It occurred to me that I'd lived so long in fear. Scared that I'd fail in my career, in love, that I'd default on my loans, disappoint my father and friends. Scared that I'd walk down the wrong street, confront the wrong person. That I'd get a speeding ticket, get caught stealing music online. There was nothing to my life but fear.

Zelda stops and sniffs at something in the vines. I hear it. A snake moving away from her. Its slither a hiss in the shadows. She gets ready to pounce when I stop her. There's no telling its size. She's become adept at snake hunting out here, but it never ceases to give me worry. When we're this far from town. This far from the truck. I could cut the wound. Suck out the venom, but still, I'd have to carry her after that. I guess I still have some worry.

These are my favorite moments. When the world of man is absent, and I hear the earth. The shifting in the trees. The whispers and calls of bugs and reptiles. Above me, pieces of moon fall through the trees. Columns. Connecting my body to that above. We ford a glimmering stream. A toad hops into ivy. They look like clumps of clay. Rusty brown, moundy muscle. Around a bend I encounter a villager spearing one. He looks to me. I nod. He smiles, dingy teeth punctuating his mouth, holds his small trident aloft, the amphibian kicking wildly. What must that be like? Thrashing the air. Knowing you've found death but not understanding how. He clears the thin path and I walk by, Zelda keeping to my right, her eye on the stranger. There is part of me that wants to turn around once we pass him, but I don't. I know it's a sign of weakness. Instead, I listen. Assess those sounds that are ours. He doesn't follow us. No strangers ever do; it's only those I know that have done me harm.

At the top of the hill, we find an overlook. There are a few lights below us. People not yet asleep. The town looks snowy in the moonlight. The ocean in the distance a plate of glass. As if on cue, sweat rolls down my temple, the illusion snuffed from me. The luminance reminds me of the snow in Kentucky. How we always wished it would snow on the holidays. Then, I think of my sister who always struggles with seasonal depression, always wants me to come home for the holiday. She will expect to hear from me, but won't.

When I do send my correspondences, I send a box to Devon in Seattle. He mails them for me, so no one knows where I am. Eventually I'll mail my brother and sister on the important days. Birthdays, Christmas, the anniversary of my father's death.

Whether or not my brother is alive, I don't know. It occurs to me that it could be cruel to mail letters to him on behalf of my sister if he's dead. It's possible that he's better. Found a job. Gotten a phone. Possible but unlikely.

Tomorrow is another day off work. I think about sleeping on the overlook. Remember that there's been a mountain lion roaming. Half mad with rabies. A boy was mauled last week. Carried away and mostly hollowed out. I check my waist for the knife. I learned some survival skills from a local hunter. He traded in beer. Still, the idea of waking to a mountain lion doesn't please me. I pet Zelda and we begin our journey back.

36

I should have seen it. The gaps in time. The escalating restlessness at night. The building mistrust. But I was lost. Someone called it trauma, but I said no, that I'd not known it to be trauma. Felt the word too serious. Too loaded. Marines experienced trauma. Watched friends killed. Innocent children, parts scattered along the streets of Kabul. Not the Forty-year-old man who's lost his father. I was just experiencing loss. Maybe she should have seen me. Seen that I wasn't right. That I couldn't remember this or that. That I couldn't be held accountable for everything because it was all spinning out of my hands. The more I tried to grasp my world, the less I could.

I'd gone to her house. When she'd all but vanished. When all of her messages had become fragments of Latin, Greek, some other language not quite known to man. She'd not let me into the house. We sat on the deck. I'd not been sleeping. Not eaten much. This is how I get. Even now. Restless. My body deprived of food. Of sleep. The world fuzzy around the edges. Words slow to form and always off key. She had dark circles beneath her eyes. Her hair crudely pulled into a knot upon her head. A squirrel nest run through with a pencil. She was usually so well put together. No hair out of place, no wear to her body. She was slow to speak. Fidgeted with a leaf that had fallen onto the table. Her eyes shifted between the lids. As if scanning a document. As if she was an android in a movie making calculations, schematics and definitions appearing on a screen inside her.

Those were the hardest moments to find language. To say the things I'd gone over in my head. Gone over aloud in the car. I fumbled with it. Stumbling into an off-center compliment. About how she looked—even when she hadn't spent hours in front of the mirror. She looked at me, head turned, as if she'd never heard such a sound. I'd expected a confrontation. A *you-shouldn't-say-that-to-a-lady*. Got nothing. Her eyes traced me. They scanned my face. Hung on the lips for a moment. Instead of a kiss, she placed a finger to them. It wasn't a soft touch. A *shhhh*. A loving touch. Emma was testing if I was real. If my skin was sturdy and true. Was this a night terror? Had I come upon her during sleep?

I pulled back. Asked what she was doing. Like I did when she was asleep. She didn't respond. Touched me again. Slightly harder. Parted my lips with her index finger and thumb. Rubbed along my gum line. Stop it, I said. I clapped my hands. Wake up, I said. She jerked but didn't speak. Didn't tell me to stop. I launched into the program. Talked about my feelings of isolation. That she'd become a phantom. Like a fool, I listed the times I'd reached out to her with no response. I asked her what her responses were about. Why she had replied with unrelated verbs or body parts. For ten minutes I did this. Worked myself into a verbal frenzy. Lost in the tow of my own emotion. My volume increasing. Up and up and faster until I said it. Until

I said what I'd tried to avoid saying. As not to put ideas in her head. As if that was possible. Are you breaking up with me?

Emma didn't move. Didn't respond. Her eyes were fixed on something inside me. I could feel it. Her eyes digging around under my skin. She stood. Turned and walked into her house. I heard the locks thrum to. The sun stabbed at me between the branches. Those weird Kentucky autumns. One day chilly and wet, the next hot and heavy. I expected her to come back out. When she didn't, I looked to the windows. Hoping she might peek between the curtains. She did not. I stood. Paced. Thought about what to do. Left.

I sat in my car for some time. Staring at the clock on my radio. It was always off. If not by five minutes, by an hour and five. It was as if it was running out of batteries. My thought kept returning to Emma. To the way she looked at me. As if I wasn't there. Or that I was there but that she was looking inside of me. Peeling my skin apart. Layer by layer. Each part of me nothing more than an onion skin.

37

I awake to laughter. A child outside my window tossing honeysuckle blooms onto me. I growl like a bear and Poco erupts into laughter. I can tell he's trying to cover his mouth, can imagine him hunched over with a hand full of flowers, his missing tooth pronounced by his boyish smile. He tossed the whole lot in, a blossoming of yellow blooms suspended for a moment in the breeze before it collapses on me. Shirtless, I run after him and we zig and zag through the huts, Zelda in tow, yipping and wagging.

Poco leads us to the shore, where he stops at the waves, and doubles back toward the cantina. Pivoting on my heel, I lose balance, and skid in a cloud of sand. Zelda, moving too fast for her own good, nearly collides with me. She jumps just in time, but lands on her side in an awkward tumble. Quick to regain composure, she comes to my aid, licking my face.

Get 'em, I say, my voice sharp to let her know her duty and she is off after Poco.

The couple in the metal band shirts are beneath a cabana. They've been watching. Is that your son, the woman asks, her hand above her eyes to ease the light.

No, I say, standing and swatting sand from my body. He's a local pirate, the scourge of the village. I'll see that he's swiftly taken to prison, I say, winking to the vacationers.

I find Poco in the cantina with Anne. Zelda is lapping at a bowl of water. Did you feed her, I say.

¿Alimentamos al perro? Anne asks.

No, he says, grinning and trying to hide his smile behind a bottle of Coke.

Los frijoles dan pedos Zelda, I say and Poco giggles and shifts on the stool as if he can't contain the brilliance of this idea. His skin is smooth, the fine hairs on his back bleached by the sun and angelic.

I tickle his ribs and say, ¡te hago dormir al lado de zelda, Poco!

With this, Poco loses all composure and nearly falls off the stool laughing. I signal for Anne to slide me a drink and sit.

We eat a breakfast of tofu, peppers, and tortillas. Poco has developed a fondness for tofu. At first, he was skeptical, but he now requests it. It doesn't ever occur to him to turn down food. He is not from a world where one has such a luxury.

¿Qué te parece una aventura? I say to Poco. He shakes his head yes.

After we eat, Poco follows me to one of the trucks and we travel back toward the hills. There is scarcely a cloud in the sky and this reminds me of an essay by Italo Calvino. It's been so long since I've thought about writing or reading that the occurrence of the memory turns my stomach at first.

¿Cómo se ve esa nube? I say and point to a small cloud just over the hills.

Poco looks at me, curiosity fingering his brow.

¿Cómo es la forma? Veo un gato. Una nube en forma de gato, I say.

His eyes go wide, full moons of pleasure, and he claps twice before saying, un mapache volador.

¡Sí, una opción mucho mejor!

The truck lumbers over a dirt road and we ford a small

river into the cover of trees. I drive as far as I can up the hill, pull the truck over, and grab a backpack with water and snacks.

¿De dónde vino eso?¿Eres mágico? He asks.

¿Mágico? I say.

Poco pulls an imaginary hat from his head, waves above it and makes to pull something out. I laugh and say, si, and do a little thing with my hands.

The day is cool yet and the animals and bugs along the hills are muted or sleeping or too scared to raise their voices. Poco and I wend our way along the trail until we reach a precipice of sorts and we sit atop a rocky edge, dangling our feet. Zelda nuzzles between us and we all stare past the brambles to the buildings now so very far away. Windows, reflect the sun in blinking, wavering, dots.

Nunca he estado tan lejos de casa. Poco's voice is much smaller than usual, metallic and minor like an old sad music box.

Home seems such a heavy word to me, some barb that's only wounded me, pulled me back whenever I strayed. Though for different reasons, Poco and I are haunted by the same thing.

Irás muy lejos, pequeño amigo. Más lejos que esto/aquí, créame.

I slip a candy bar from my backpack and hand it to him. He takes it and leans against me. Zelda, crouching now, bolts off into the bushes and wakes the world.

38

Sometimes I remember things. Soft around the edges. Saturated and analog. Other times they're bright. Hard edged. Unforgiving. Digital. Events too. Some soft. Others bright and burning through me. When I think of Chelsea and Emma playing in the park or cuddling on the floor or wrestling with a hank of rope, the memory sears the toughest part of me.

They said Chelsea didn't suffer. But no one could say for certain. Before things got bad. Before Emma found her secret language. Parsed the world. I could have said I knew. But I guess at that time, it wouldn't have happened. She loved Chelsea so much. It was impossible for me to dampen that. To soften the lines. I attempted to chase the thought from my head. When it crept in, I'd run. I'd read. Write. Whatever it took. When that didn't help, I walked to the bar. I'd talk to strangers. I wanted to do things that were bad for me. I wanted to sleep with people. Take handfuls of pills. Pick up drinking. Instead, I starved myself. Ate less and less. Ran more and more.

I was collecting my own words. Dormant until I could learn to use them. Things that rested in the curves of my ear. My spine. The back of my throat. Bits of this and that. Waiting to be coughed out. To infect others. Fill them with shadows.

Images of foxes sneaking across misty fields with bloody cats hanging from their jaws. Things that wanted to be moved to new places and released. To spread. Arch. Bloom.

I would, later, find myself using them. Feeling them slip past my lips. Wet and warm. Their tails whipping at the edges of my teeth. In bars. Dimly lit. Friends talking around me. I was just some shadow creeping in the booth. Hunched over. A drink in my fingers. Ice melting. MRSA, I would say. Conseco, I would say. All manner of things that were collecting.

Emma got lost. Lost in skipping words. Lost in the funhouse of her concepts. She was angry about Juliana. And so it began to emerge. The dark language. Fits and starts. At the time, I couldn't recognize it. I was reeling. The further I got from the death, the more I began to remember. Slowly. Too slowly.

I had to remind myself that I had tried. Some days I would drive to her house with lunch to surprise her. I would make her vegan baked goods. I would stand in my impossibly small kitchen. Over the flame. Stir. Mix. Pour. Make. Cut. Sweating. I wrote her letters. I labored over them. Moving adverbs around. Deleting them. Weighing the sentences. Crossing them out. Writing on new pieces of paper until I'd gotten it right. As close to right as I was capable. I'd write her stories by hand. I'd saddle stitch them by hand with waxen thread. Design a cover she'd like. Letter press it. Austere. I'd search online to find her rare books. Have them delivered. I did what I could to prove to her that I loved her. That I had moved home for her. Again and again, I was met with silence. Her car would be in the driveway, but she wouldn't answer the door. Once I thought I heard her.

I leaned into the door. My hand cupped against glass. Maybe I saw her crawling. Maybe I didn't.

After her parents found her and the dog, parsed, labeled and putrefying, there was no way back, and I was told in no uncertain terms that it was my fault, and I was all too willing to believe it. I could have been more understanding the first time we tried to date. I could have not dated Juliana. I could have moved earlier. I. Could. Have. Done. Anything. Those thoughts were a dim choir of hornets. Moving around my head. Buzzing and stinging and rotting mid-air. A pitter-patter of their bodies falling.

My friends tried to convince me to see a therapist. You cannot take this on, they told me. But I didn't want to go. Eventually someone said that I should go to talk about my father. Maybe they were just trying to get me in the door, hopeful that the rest would come out too, but the trick worked. I found myself agreeing. Maybe part of me knew better, knew that I needed the help, knew that I couldn't carry the guilt for Emma much longer, so I saw a shrink.

He was gentle. Ran a late night jazz radio program. Loved the Dodgers. I'd lie on his couch. Some days unable to speak. I'd collapse on his floor in fits of anxiety. He'd walk me through breathing exercises. Tell me to focus on the trees outside the window. Change the subject when I was slipping. Talk about Jazz records. Bring me back around when I was ready.

When the freelance work dried up. When I turned to loans and credit and friends and food stamps. When I'd hide in the belly of winter for days without speaking to anyone. He began doing the therapy for free. Calling me to make sure I came. When I'd try to force the conversation, he'd carefully bring it back around to Emma, to my panic attacks at night, to my growing obsession with proving to Emma's family that I was innocent, that I was good.

I'd lie on his floor some days. He'd ask me questions. I'd answer. He'd draw my life on a map. Circles connected by lines. All my relationships. My father and mother crossed through. A tunnel no longer viable for travel. He told me that the mourning of my father was under siege. That I'd have to deal with the feelings of Emma and then my father. That Emma had bound them together. That the living was complicating the dead. So, I spoke. About the gathering of silence. The collection of space. He was quiet for a time, his eyes closed. I thought perhaps he'd nodded off. Something in me wanted to step out quietly, but didn't. Then he spoke, there seems to be a pattern you've developed.

Pattern, I asked, almost in a whisper as the question felt foolish.

Your mother, he said.

You know how I feel about Freud.

Hear me out, he said. What did you tell me about your memory of your mother?

I had a complicated relationship with it, I said.

Undoubtedly because you had a complicated relationship with

her as a child. Your entire family for that matter. You were at once the child and the caretaker.

Codependency 101, I said, anger fingering my throat slightly. Why the sudden irritation, I couldn't say.

He stood and reheated his coffee in a microwave. Apologized, said something about his late nights, then said, how does this paint your relationships?

I knew what he was going for. I'd thought it a thousand times. Playing out the family dynamic by trying to save people, wounded birds as my father once called them.

Emma is different, I said. I fucked this one up. I fucked this up somehow.

Don't jump ahead, he said, what was it you saw in Emma when you first met?

She was quiet. Seemed mousey when we first met.

Would you say she's healthy? He took his mug out of the microwave.

No, but neither am I.

You didn't cause this. You couldn't have caused this. Are you perhaps a part of the environmental factors that caused the break, that's debatable, but her path was set many years before you met her.

What do I do, I asked, almost as if pleading.

Shut the door. Shut the door on this relationship.

I found myself crying. I could feel it coming and there was nothing I could do about it. Like sick. From the root of me.

39

Anne is asleep in my bed. The melted silver of moon running along her shoulder blades. Hardening and going black in small pockets between her ribs. Her skin a river, brown, long and curving, the surface reflecting the moon, begging me to slip inside. Swim. I pull my shirt off. Grab a blanket from the shelf. Spread it on the floor. Lie upon it. Zelda comes to my side, spoons me.

When the sun wakes me, Anne is staring over the edge of the bed. Her chin propped on the seam of the thin mattress. I watch the hank of black hair droop from behind her ear and fall along her jaw line. She reminds me of those photos I'd seen in *National Geographic* as a child. Afghan women, their skin smooth, eyes piercing green. Before the wars pocked their faces with shrapnel, the sun ravaged their skin. The land dehydrated and wrinkled them.

Did you go into the hills again, she asks.

I nod.

She reaches down to touch my face. I jerk away. Something I've always done.

Were you hit as a boy, she asks.

Was I beat up, or a fight?

Abused by a parent or something?

No. My parents weren't violent.

Exactly what an abused kid would say. She laughs, turns onto her back and looks at the ceiling. Says, when are you going to lay with me?

I stand. Walk to the sink. Wash my face. Look at Anne in the mirror. She's let the sheet gather around her waist. Her loveliness not lost on me. Some days I want to swim.

There was a kid when I was growing up, I say, he was beautiful. In the summers, his skin tanned without burning. His eyes, blue, clear. He went to my school. Later joined my swim team. I was in Group Three. The slow group. Little kids and kids my age who didn't really have what it took to swim competitively. The young ones were hopefuls. The rest of us were just paychecks. Athletic babysitting. Jason was in Group One. He won ribbons. An Olympian in training. In school, he'd grab the asses of the girls in the halls. Say things like, tush inspection. The girls took to calling him Hollywood. He was my friend at first. You know, when he first moved to town. But I soon realized that despite his family's wealth, his looks, his skills as an athlete, he was a chronic liar. He'd come by my house and look at my room. Flip through the records of bands he didn't know. Read my fanzines. Go to school the next day bragging about his new Buzzcocks record, his skateboard, whatever. I didn't talk about that shit back then. It was my life, you know? People at school didn't need to know I wasn't like them. That I didn't like Michael Jackson or Phil Collins or whatever. Then he took to making fun of me. Telling people I wanted to be like him.

I stop and look down at my hands. The water still dripping off of them.

What does that have to do with anything, she asks.

I don't know anything about you, Anne. But I get the sense that you come from money. That the thing you're running from down here is your future. The burden of the good life.

You've got me all figured out, huh, she says.

Objection fingers her face into arcs and curves. I know I'm supposed to rethink and phrase things carefully. I'm supposed to comfort her. I turn around. Lean against the sink.

Yeah, my parents have money, she says, but I'm here for other reasons.

Winners have no business messing with people like me, I say.

That's a sad way to look at the world, she says.

I expect her to storm out. To say something hurtful.

Well, she says, stepping out of the sheet and onto the floor exposing her lean body, I aim to prove you wrong.

I nod. Slip on a shirt. Head to work. Maybe Emma was right. Maybe my sadness *does* fill rooms.

Today I'm cooking. It's my least favorite duty. The onion works my eyes. Catches in my throat. Fiery and jagged. I tried goggles. Nose and mouth guards. Somehow it always gets to me. Slim is already working on the beans. Stirring them. Adding spices. He knows I can't take the onions. Arrives early to ensure I'll have to cut them. He's been here longer so I don't object. I pull a crate of yellows. Wonder if they're indigenous. In Seattle, there's always a push for local and natural. Down here, it's different. They grow what they can to export.

I take one into my hand. Trace the ridges with my finger. Two thoughts come to me. The first a surgeon who was in an intro to drawing class I took during my freshman year in college. He came in the second night with fine line drawings of onions so true to life they'd make my eyes water. Mine were crude attempts at cow skulls that roused laughs from the art students. The second, an aging Australian man I met in a hostel in Kassel. We talked over bread and jam. He pulled an onion from his backpack, peeled away the dry top layer, and took a bite. Eat it whole, he said. It's the key to a long life.

That and lovemaking, he joked. The bursts of juice caught the rising sunlight. The beads running down his leathery chin.

I begin peeling and chopping. I don't wipe my eyes. I don't walk away sniffling. The tears and snot come freely, but I raise my chin to ensure they don't fall into the pile of chop. When I finish, I scrape them into a stainless steel box. Clear my face with a towel. Throw it at Slim.

One day, my friend, you won't be the new guy, he says.

You're wrong, I say.

About?

I'm not your friend.

Slim laughs.

My body burns. Nearly blinded by tears, I stagger to the open-air showers. Lower my head and run the cold water over me. With time, I feel better. Return to the kitchen. Slim is chopping potatoes. I know little about him. Once he told me that he'd gotten his name when he was in North Dakota driving cattle. So thin at the time a gust of wind blew him off a horse. He claims it wasn't the wind as much as it was his falling asleep at the saddle. Even today he must weigh a buck twenty-five wet.

These people are drifters. One year crab fishermen in Alaska, the next picking fruit in New York. There are no lasting relationships. People are just stories waiting to be plucked when ripe and carried away. I will be in his oral history and he is in my book.

When my shift ends, I join Anne at the bar. She slides a beer in front of me.

You know I don't drink, I say.

She smiles and says, I suppose I'll have to drink this then.

You seen Poco today?

She shakes her head. Slides me a bottle of cold water.

Do you want children, she asks.

No.

I think you'd take Poco home with you if you could.

I look to her. Her smile, aligned teeth. This is home, I say.

She shakes her head. None of us live here, she says, we just borrow it.

I know she's right. Neither she nor I are true to drifting. We are only visitors. She'll go home eventually. To the gaudy houses and social obligations. I'll end up somewhere else. Some city down here where I'll buy a home with the money I've saved. The benefits of making American wages in Mexico.

She reaches over the bar. Kisses me. I don't open my mouth. She backs away.

One day, she says.

You only want me because I don't chase you around like these other guys.

Yeah, she says, at first.

I leave the bar. Let Zelda out of my room. We walk to the beach and sit under our tree.

40

When I heard the news, I drove directly to Emma's house and then to her parents'. The house was empty, its windows dark and sinister as if the ghosts of past generations lurked just behind the glass and pleaded for me to leave. Instead, I sat on a porch swing and waited—patiently beyond the sinking of the stubborn sun, beyond the rise of the humid gloom, deep into the night when I'd become scarcely more than a litanous network of bug bites. Slowly, her father's SUV crept along the serpentine drive, its lights striking my eyes painfully. As they descended from the final hill and fell upon me, washing me out in their luminance, I stood from the bench and approached the walkway to greet them. Emma's mother did not emerge from the car, but her father did and met me at the conflux of the walkways and the drive.

We can't have you coming around, son, he told me. His use of the son was not paternal but dismissive, reductive, as if he were marking the distance between their blood and mine. Though old, he was not a slight man. He loomed over me, backlit, his face slightly obscured by shadow. I don't mean to intrude, I said, I'm confused and no one will talk to me. He angled his head, perhaps a tick of sympathy, perhaps not, and said, you had your time to talk with Emma, now she needs to be around her family. Can you just tell me, I began. No, he interrupted, I can't tell you anything. Does she blame me, I said. I'm not sure why I asked this, but I did, and was given the blunt edge of its comeuppance. If a guy has to ask that, he said, he has the answer.

Her dad pivoted to his left on one foot and raised his arm to let me know that I was then expected to leave, which I did. Before I made it to my car, I turned and asked if they'd let me know what I could do, to which he very quickly offered that I'd done enough.

That drive from the farm was the darkest and longest trip I remember taking. It was as if the trees were bending down to hit the roof of my car, as if every manner of creature came scurrying in front of me, as if every pothole was drained of its sand and tar and opened wide for my tires. I played the conversation out in my mind. Moved it back and forth, considered nuances of body language, tested alternate answers I could have offered, but none of it made sense. There was in my heart a coil of anger that trembled inside me. Made my hands sweat. Caused my throat to close in. There were no clear thoughts any longer. Fragments of ideas flipped inside the dim soup of my confusion and sank to more dismal regions where they operated below the horizon of language, where I couldn't rationalize them. I could only feel them as an ache.

41

It's been days since I've seen Poco. It's not typical. On my day off, I wake early and leave Zelda with Anne. Pack a bag with some food and Cokes. A shadow slings along the ridges of my spine and I reach for some medical supplies.

I don't know where he lives, so I go into to the village and begin asking around at the local shops. It had never occurred to me to take a photo of the kid. Now I wish that I had. At one of the stores I ask if they have a camera. The man gives a small laugh. Tells me no. When I reach a row of small homes, I begin knocking on doors. At one, I'm met by an old woman. Her fingers knotted and swollen. Long years of working fields. Of knitting. Of working. I think of my mother. Of her reedy fingers. Not a callous on them.

Disculpe, busco a un chico. Es así de alto, I say, raising my hand to the approximate height of Poco. Viene a menudo al albergue en la playa. Lleva una camiseta Federación Mexicana. Lleva una camisa Mexicana Federación.

She looks at me, her eyes wet, nearly pulpy inside the lids. Hay muchos niños en esta aldea, She says, lo siento, pero no puedo ayudarte.

I thank her and continue down the street, moving away from the brightly painted buildings of town center, past the stores with illuminated open signs in their windows, and find myself in that area where the old migrant workers from the days of the coffee trade lived in the off seasons. The temporary homes were not built to accommodate families, but now they often house extended families of the farmers and fishermen in the area. Some of the homes sit crookedly upon their foundations, their corners creeping into the hardened earth. I begin knocking on doors. Most go unanswered. I cross through a public square where a fountain, which doesn't seem to have worked for decades, sits kingly amid a well-manicured park. It's austere save for the occasional gust of wind kicking up dust into thin spirals. I sit beneath the shade of a tree. Drink some water. In the distance, I hear children playing. Their voices, spikey and uneven, reflecting off buildings, snaking through streets. They seem to come from the southern part of the village. I walk to the church, find them playing tag in the lawn. When I approach them, one of the boys, roughly the age of Poco, or at least what I think his age is, comes over to me.

¿Te has perdido?

No. Busco a mi amigo. Un muchacho de tu edad. Lleva una una camiseta Federación Mexicana.

The boy calls to a girl. Talks to her for a moment. Looks back to me. He says, su nombre es Arturo. Vive con su abuela por el bosque. Es la única casa por allí.

I thank them. Pull two candy bars from my bag. Tell the kids to hide them so the others don't see. They run around the corner of the church to eat their candy undisturbed.

The woods to the west of town are dense, but a few scattered homes, mostly empty, pepper the fringe. In the first house I approach, there is a keyless piano in a room, the floor, sunken through with rain. Vines hang through a hole in the ceiling. A stray dog, curled in the corner, his scruff tangled in dried mud, looks up. I move to the next house. A man, about my age, comes to the door. I inquire, he tells me to try a faded pink house about a mile down the way.

Behind the buildings, a wretch of a dog follows. Keeping to the shadows, he only reveals himself in the gaps between homes, where the faded grass leans with the wind. Many of the homes look abandoned, but more than once, the face of a small child blooms in the darkened gaps between window slats.

In the door well, a warped door, something taken from another place, a much shorter building, hangs loosely from a couple hinges. I knock and the door wobbles. At first there is no reply. I knock again. Harder but not hard enough to rattle the thing from the jamb. I call out. Hola. Hola. I hear a light reply. A woman's weak voice.

¿Puedo pasar y hablar con usted?

Sí.

To open the door, I must lift the knob, angle the wood, push, holding it steady so that it doesn't fall from the hinges. There are two doors on the far end of the house. One has a sheet draped over it. The other is open. In the dark, I make out a pale face, dimpled and old. Her hair upon her head in a bun. When I am closer, I smell her. Urine and shit. She sits in a bed. A gray woolen blanket over her legs.

I ask her if she's okay. She says she can't move. She tells me the boy stopped coming to help her. I ask if his name is Arturo. Si, she says, sí. A good boy she tells me. It's all I can do to breathe in the room. So dark. So vile.

¿Vive aquí?

Sí.

She asks if I can help her. I tell her I will. I tell her that I want to check on the boy. She nods. Closes her eyes. When I leave the room, she coughs. Says something I can't quite make out. I go to the next room. Pull back the dirty sheet in the doorway. Arturo is on the bed. His skin luminescing with sweat. It's hard to tell if he's breathing. His chest looks still. I kneel. Feel his head. Fever. Lean over. Place my ear to his chest. Hear a faint rattling breath. Arturo, I say. My voice soft. He doesn't reply. Doesn't open his eyes.

Poco, I say. Goddmamn it, Poco, I whisper. My throat burns. My face goes hot. I pull my shirt off. Pour water on it. Wet his body. Remove his shorts. The stink of him nearly too much. I tear the sheet from the doorway. Pour water on it. Wash him clean. When I'm lifting his small genitals, his eyes open. Barely.

Arturo, estoy aquí. No te preocupes.

A thin smile.

From the medicine bag, I pull out a bottle of amoxicillin. Crush a pill with the gritty edge of a cola bottle. I use a tin cup from the front room to mix orange drink with the medicine. Prop his head up with my hand. Help him drink it down. He frowns. Whispers, *ick*. I remember being a boy. Sipping the pink penicillin from a spoon. My neck spasming in disgust afterward. Only a few more, my mother would say, then give me a Ginger-Ale.

In the sink, I wash his shorts. His underwear. His shirt. His sheets. Hang them to dry on the window ledge. I return to the old woman. Scrape the waste from her mattress. Ask her if it's okay for me to wash her. She tells me that Arturo speaks of me. That he sometimes brings her the Cokes I give him. I pull her soiled gown over her head. She's not wearing under garments. I tear the sheet from her window. Soak it. Begin wiping her clean. Her flesh reminds me of my father's. How it hangs about her body. Puckered, stretched, and dimpled. She smiles at me. Apologizes for her nudity. Thanks me. I strip the sheets, rolling her from side to side. Take everything to the sink. Soak it in water.

I check back in on Arturo. He's curled in the center of his

mattress. Shivering. I call his name but he's asleep. I want to cuddle behind him. Hold him. Keep his body from shivering. Will the illness from his body. The old woman calls to me from her room.

Señor, señor, she says.

Sí, I say. Walking around the rickety table and chairs. A pall of dirt kicks up outside the window. A dog barks somewhere close by. How long have they lived like this? The boy essentially on his own. When I get to her, she's trying to sit up.

Me siento expuesta.

Es sólo por un rato. Se están secando.

She frowns. I understand. I'd hate to be naked and immobile as well. I give her some food. A drink. Explain to her what's happening. The clothes need drying. I need to get supplies. The boy is very ill. He needs care. Worry holds her face.

Pensé que se fue. Al igual que su madre, she says.

42

Life it seems is about loss. We collect it. Gather it in our pockets so we can pull it out later under the pale sunlight and admire it. Some of these losses are expected. For example, as my father once explained it, most people shed their childhood friends rather early in life. I didn't believe him. Thought they'd last forever. We stood by each other. Built forts. Killed bugs. Rode bikes in the creamy sunsets. Played 8-bit video games together. He was right though. Those friendships wouldn't last past eighth grade. Moving, school changes, girls. Some days I couldn't even remember their names. They'd been replaced with other friends. Some of which stayed with me into my forties, others who didn't. Then there are losses that are unexpected. Those losses that come far before anticipated. Break ups, suicides, accidents.

I was used to losing people. People came and went. Some stayed longer than others. I'd learned to give up on most of my family. Their addictions too strong. Before my father sobered up, I'd nearly given up on him. Fortunately, he'd had a heart attack when I was nineteen, and he was forced to quit drinking. Losing people had become too consistent. Somewhere in my head, a secret gear, spinning without hinder, generated anxiety. An unknown fear. So, I had developed a pattern of abandoning people, sometimes too early. It was a reaction, one I'd never have seen without help.

I could barely process the loss of my father and I wasn't ready to lose Emma.

I'd sit in the apartment and look at photos of her. Maybe if it hadn't come immediately after my father's death, I could've processed it. Processed one or the other. But two points, knotted and ugly, ripped me in opposite directions. No manner of thought helped me. There was no reason to death or to the chaos of my heart. Perhaps the pressure of my affection was too great.

Fuck you, I said. Zelda looked up from the couch. Not, you, I cooed. I took to pacing again. I walked the floors. Tapped the walls. The dog watching, hoping for a walk. She crawled off her couch and followed. We paced around the room until I forgot we were pacing. Forgot I was moving and tripped over her after a quick turn. It was raining outside. Always seemed to be raining at that time. A terrible hot rain. I stepped outside. Zelda in tow. The fringed machete of her tail wagging. I wanted to break everything but couldn't lift my arms. I looked to Zelda who sat at the edge of the porch watching the rain. Looked into her mismatched eyes. She licked my chin. Goddamn it, I said, I'm so fucking sorry.

This was what happened in break ups. People assumed blame that was not necessarily all theirs. They forgot the bad things and remembered the good. The walks and kisses and presents and laughter. They forgot the jealousy and fighting and uncomfortable silent car rides. But was this a break up? Yes, it most certainly was. I thought about the signs that I should've recognized. The labeling. The secret language. The splitting of reason. The night terrors. The things I chose to find charming.

I loaded Zelda into the car. Drove to Lexington. Sat outside Emma's house. Not sure what prompted me to go. What it was to mean. I wanted it to be different. Wanted her to be there. Wanted Chelsea and Zelda to play. To bite around each other's hindquarters and yip and growl. It began getting dark. The sun never leaving the cloudbank. Everything already shadows. I let Zelda out to pee. She ran to the door instead. I chased her. Emma's neighbor stepped outside. Made small talk. Asked where Emma had been. On vacation, I lied. The grass is getting long, the old woman complained. Without thinking about it, I went into Emma's garage. Pulled out her mower. Cut the grass. I put the clippings into the trash. Dragged it to the curb. She would know this somehow. Her neighbor would tell her parents. They would tell her. She'd see that it wasn't my fault. That I was a good man. I was a good man.

While in town, I went to Emma's favorite coffee shop. Some part of me hoped they'd recognize me. That they'd tell me some update about Emma I'd not heard. This wasn't the case. They didn't know me. They smiled at the dog. Gave her a treat. Served me a tea too hot for any mouth. I sat at Emma's favorite table. Looked at the fliers wheat-pasted to the wall. Recalled the conversations we'd had about the old local plays. Which ones had her ex-boyfriend acted in? When she and I were teens and her ex was hardly a man? Zelda nosed between my legs. Rested her chin on the chair. I knew there was a limited window for my tea. A couple minutes between too hot and too cold. I monitored it with a keen eye. Emma had teased me about this. My tea window. You're too particular, she'd said. I was already putting her into the past tense. It weighed on me more than I expected. I left the tea on the table. Took Zelda to the car. Sat in silence for a time.

43

Devon gives me permission to move Poco and his grandmother into a bungalow for a while. I ask Anne to help me. I grab a folding cot from storage. Lay two twin mattresses on the floor of the hostel's cargo van. Cover them in sheets. Anne hops into the passenger seat. We drive across town. When we arrive at the small, slat board house, I ease the van back toward the front door. The ground is cracked and dry where faint grooves had been formed by rivulets of rainwater. It's been weeks since we've seen a drop. The shocks wheeze at the imbalance.

Inside, the old woman calls for me. ¿Es usted? I tell her that it is. That I've brought a friend to help. Poco is asleep in his room. He is once again covered in sweat. He looks dead. His dark skin gone beige. I wrap him in a beach towel and carry him to the van. His eyes open. Slightly. His body barely weighs into the mattress. Among the bleached white sheets, he is a stain. I'm staring. Motionless. Anne walks out of the house.

You weren't kidding, man. That place is bleak.

Yeah, I say. Not moving my eyes from the thinline body in the van. I'll need help with the old woman. I say, pulling out the folded cot from the side of the mattress.

We help the old woman sit up and cover her in a sheet. I wrap my arms around her chest; Anne gathers her feet. She doesn't go to the cot easily. It's as if she's scared of it.

¡Cuidado! ¡Cuidado!

Claro, I say.

She begins to tremble, twist. I wrap tighter. Trying to keep her steady. When I lean right, she shifts right. When I adjust left, she follows. Each time, Anne's fingers move farther apart. A bead of sweat runs between my eyes and my nose ignites with an itch. Just as she's about to break my finger lock, we get her to the cot. Anne tells her to be very still. To trust us. We lift, Anne exaggerating a grunt. The wooden frame creaks and moans as we waddle the old woman through the house. It takes some effort, but I'm able to push the cot across the top of one of the mattresses. Poco looks over to his grandmother, his eyes slivers between lids. She reaches over to him.

Mi Arturo. Mi Arturo, she says. A waxing toothless smile born above her chin.

Should we take their clothes, Anne asks.

No, I say, closing the van doors, I'm going to buy them new things.

Anne goes for the front door. I tell her to mind the shape. That the door will dehinge if she moves it wrong.

She fusses with it for a couple moments. Considers the angles. Closes it without much trouble.

✺

The sun is low on the horizon. Its glow painting the room in Princeton orange. Both Poco and the old woman are sleeping. Her chest heaves as she snores. His is nearly motionless. Death is trying to claim him. I watch the shadows gather on his body. I want to wipe him clear of them. My breath gets deeper. My heart is rage. I've been sitting here for two hours. Waiting for the doctor to arrive. This is not Seattle, I tell myself. There is no immediacy, here. I turn the overhead light on. The shadows clear from Poco. I watch his chest. Rise, I say, so quietly I can barely hear it. Outside, the world continues. The waves push and pull. A couple is out there. The woman running into the water. She's yelling to her partner, Baby, the water feels so good. Join me. Join me. He doesn't speak. Come on, baby. Part of me wants to stand up and look out the window. See the couple on the beach. The woman in the waves. The man drinking in a chair. The cool customer. Unable to enjoy the moment with her. I'd never seen Poco play in the water. He'd once thrown Zelda's ball into the ocean for her. When she'd bring it back, her wet tail thrashing, he'd laugh and toss it again. He never once entered it. Not so much as a toe touching the hushed fringe that crept, slowed, and retreated to the deep. Perhaps he didn't know how to swim. No one to teach him.

I smell the tiki torches outside. Imagine the black smoke rising from the flames. The old woman coughs in her sleep. She moves her arms, bunches covers beneath her armpit. Who will look after Poco when she dies? I laugh. One of those laughs I don't expect. Like a cough. Who will take care of her if Poco dies? The thought comes so naturally that it catches me off guard. A jab in my lungs. A world without Poco.

You should take a break, Anne says.

I wasn't aware she was in the doorway. I'm okay, I tell her. I want to wait for the doctor.

She leans against the jamb. Crosses her arms. Looks over her shoulder toward the pool. I guess you're in luck, she says. As she moves from the doorway, an old man limps in. Nodding at her then to me.

Is this the boy, he asks, his English broken.

What took you so long?

Many people to see, he says, opening a small bag and removing his stethoscope.

Anne is scowling at me. She mouths, *chill the fuck out.* I do my best to scowl at her. She rolls her eyes like a teen. The doctor attempts to sit on the edge of Poco's bed.

Here, I say, scooting a chair toward him. Sit.

He thanks me. Sits. Begins listening to Poco's chest. Feels around his throat. Taps his stomach. Parts the boy's eyelids. Looks at his eyes. Removes an otoscope from his bag. Looks in Poco's ears. Slips a thermometer in his ear. Looks at the reading. There's a moment where the doctor stares out of the window, as if transfixed by the stars. He sighs and looks at me.

His fever is very high. We will need ice.

That won't break the fever, Anne says.

The doctor responds to me without looking at her. Is your friend the doctor?

I say, no.

Ice, he says, will break the fever.

She's right, I say. He will shiver. It increases body temperature.

Are you a doctor?

No, I say. I know it's no use. I say, okay, we'll get ice.

Anne looks at me. I give a nod. A nod that signifies that we're not going to use ice. I look at the old man. What is it? What does the boy have?

I see this all day, he answers, virus. You should have called sooner.

I just found him ill today.

Escarlatina. He's been ill sometime. Too long. The next day is important. He will make it, or he won't. He touches Poco's hand. Pats it. Have you given him medicine?

I've given him some amoxicillin.

The doctor pulls out a small bottle from his bag. Sets it on the nightstand between the two beds. He looks at Poco's grandmother. Is she sick, he asks.

No.

Give the boy these pills. Every eight hours. About twelve days. The doctor gets up from the chair. Asks us to join him outside. We follow. He asks to be paid. I know he's marked up the pills. It's still cheaper than in the States. Anne starts to haggle but I stop her. I hand him some bills. Before I let go of them, I say, this covers the follow up you'll give next week. Understood? The old doctor looks a little frustrated, but nods in agreement.

He steps away but stops. Frowns. Says, I no think he make it. But my prayers...

He turns the corner and Anne says, his fucking prayers? She touches my arm, don't listen to him.

He's right.

About?

Poco is really sick. And.

And what, Anne asks, trying to pull my arm into her hands.

I want to tell her that everything I love dies. That I watch them fade away. Watch their breath collapse inside their bodies. Never to rise again. But I don't. I step into the bungalow and wipe the boy with a cool damp towel. He wakes. His eyelids barely parting. He gives me a thin smile.

¿Quieres un refresco?

He whispers, Sí.

I crush some medicine. Sprinkle it in a cup. Pour in grape drink. Mix it. Prop up his head. Poco sips it. Slowly at first but quicker after a few seconds.

¿Te gusta el sabor de uva?

He pauses. Swallows. Nods.

When he's finished, I tuck him into the sheets. I leave a bottle of water by his side. Tell him to sip it whenever he wakes up. Tell him that Anne and I won't leave his side. To sleep and have sweet dreams. His eyes close and he sleeps.

44

Jim stopped by. Asked me to lunch. Offered to pay. It was sunny but the rainwater filled gutters and alleys. The black water looked as if it could become something else. Had some creature lurking just beneath. Like the swamp water I'd seen as a boy. The swamps down south where my grandfather had taken me fishing. Something I barely remembered. I could remember the boat. The hat my grandfather had worn. Little else.

Jim tapped on the steering wheel. Sang a song that was really a combination of songs. He didn't know that he was singing. Didn't know that he was tapping and adjusting the volume knob when the stereo wasn't on. Jim was thinking about work. Thinking about cancer research. Saving lives. On his best days, it grated my nerves, but that day it tore at them, dug to their cores. I said nothing. Reached over, turned the power on. I'm doing it again, Jim said. It's okay, I said. I don't know why I do it, he said. Maybe you're trying to find the two songs you're singing, I said. Two, he asked. One's Michael Jackson; the other is Prince, I said. Oh, Jim said, rubbing his knuckle across his nose. I know it drives you crazy. Un poco, I said. Si, he said and laughed. Then, he paused for a thought and asked, do you think Emma's parents will let you visit her? It was a question I'd asked myself ten times a day. I looked out into the traffic and said, I don't know if anyone knows I exist anymore, Jim. I think I'm just a footnote to her life. You said her dad liked you, he said. Allegedly, I said. Her mom, Jim asked. Never met her, I began, and it doesn't matter anyway. They're busy trying to find out how this could happen to two women in the family. I'm sure my name didn't even come up. There was a moment where the song on the radio, something from the seventies, a song about animals and love, filled the car. When it ended, Jim asked, who's blaming you?

A car ran a red light. Almost clipped Jim's car. I was a loaded spring of knees and elbows. Forgot the question. Jim asked again. Later, over a bed of rice and curried tofu. I stared at the yellow grains of rice. The specks of red catching the overhead lights. I remembered Emma sitting across the same table months previously. How she had prodded me about my word choice. For a moment, it was almost as if she was there. Her friends. They think I was cheating on her, I said. Why do they think that, he asked. I didn't know, I suppose because she told them as much. He asked me if I did. No, I said, I suppose I wasn't present enough to love her the way she needed. Or maybe it's because I'd lied to her before. Shit, maybe because every time Juliana came up, I just blanked. I could tell Jim was drifting into his own thoughts but he caught himself and said, why do you think that is? My memory wasn't great, I began, but I also panicked. Jim stopped eating. His chopsticks hovered between his plate and mouth. I can't believe she did it, he said, I know it's true, but I still can't believe it.

Somewhere in the back of the restaurant glasses rattled. It

became a static that overwhelmed me. Deafening me to anything. Making my stomach soft. My heart caged and vicious. I stood and left the building.

✺

There's a video. A guy sets himself on fire. He runs through the streets. No one looks at him. He runs until his body quits him. Then he burns a bit longer. All things human, inhuman. Black, wrinkled, glistening ooze. I thought about this when I couldn't fall asleep at night. When I was a boy, I thought of things I wanted to do. Thought of the fun I'd had in the day. I thought about things that made me happy. Put me at ease.

I wanted to remember the good times but could only remember death. I could only remember the frailty of the body in that hospital bed. The funeral service had been a collection of all the good memories. The cherry pick. But even then, it was to chase away the memory of the shallow breathing. Of the wires and tubes and shit and stench. I began to bury it all. After the funeral, I thought of Emma. I thought of the things left to do. Of putting one foot before the next. Of the march away from Seattle. However, even that grew difficult, as the few good memories we'd shared were being replaced by her secret language, her absence, her process of cutting away the world and parsing each internal organ. Soon, there were no good memories left.

I tried to visit. To write letters. To talk to her parents again. Her friends. Anyone who was in touch with her. No one would have it. A strong front. You're no good for her. You've caused this. I began to look back. Roll through messages. Emails. Reread letters from Juliana. Searching for anything that I may have missed. Some word that implicated me. I talked to my therapist. Lay upon his floor. Always, he told me to close the door. To move on. Open another door later. Nothing helped. No amount of reading or writing or talking. I walked the streets at night. As the weather turned from hot to cold. The cool autumn never lasting. I sat on a bench outside my father's apartment. Tried to force myself to think of him. Of his soap collection. Of the way he laughed at his own jokes. Of his piles of mail and pills and calendar pages he'd saved because the images were pleasing. But they were just sentences. In my heart I couldn't feel anything. It was dead to everything but the anxiety of Emma. Trembling between chambers. A hungry worm. Chewing and chewing. Making more space for itself. Until I woke up one Saturday. The grass frosted from cold. I called Devon. Told him I'd take him up on his offer. I'd pack my bags. Load my car. What of the dog? What of immigration? What of this of that? There are ways around officials, he told me. There are things we can do. People we can pay. It's not much.

Most of my things I donated to charity. Some things I put in storage. Nice things I sold to secure my passage with the dog. I left my apartment without notice. Left the keys in the empty living room. Taped a note to the door.

45

I leave the store with four bags of clothing. It's likely more than the two have ever owned. At first, I wonder if this is tacky. To give them so much. But decide I don't care. I want them to have enough. More than enough. Something feels as if it's vibrating in me. A sense. Fingers along my neck or something. I'm being stalked. I turn around. See nothing at first, but then, a dog. I walk a little farther and turn to see the black stray is following me along the road. He's part wolf. His ears pointed. A plume of fur upon his chest. He's starving. His ribs, shining stripes. Hipbones poking beneath his leathery skin. I stop. Face him. His eyes lost. Recessed into him. Pitch and dull. More beast than companion. I approach him, my hand out. Bags dangling from my arms all sway and hiss. He growls. Lowers his head. He backs away from me. I pull a piece of fried dough from one of the bags. Lay it upon the hard earth. The dog does not eat the bread. He steps past it. His lips above his teeth.

You are death, I tell him. You won't follow me home.

I continue walking and the stray follows. I want to kick him. To send him yipping into the dusty afternoon light. Into the hills to hunt doe and finch. I haven't the villainy in me. We arrive at a field blocked off by a wooden fence. The boards rotting with age, but sturdy enough to keep the dog at bay. I toss the bags over. Then, I leap over, my hand on the top. Careful not to break the beam with my weight. The dog growls on the other side. Paces back and forth. I dig into my grocery bag. Find a small round of cheese. Peel away the paper. Break it in half. Drop it on the ground. The dog sniffs. Looks to me. Snatches the cheese and skulks away.

Even if it's just for tonight, Poco will live. I will stand in the door. Board the windows. Chase shadows from the corners and block black-eyed dogs from carrying him away in their jaws. When I arrive at the hostel, Anne is carrying a tray of food to the bungalow. Tortillas, chili, rice, beans, bits of banana chopped. She tells me that she's made a plate for me too. In the heat, it seems impossible to crave anything. I step into the kitchen and slip some liquefied flavored ice treats in the freezer. They remind me of my father. When I took ill, he always bought me Monster Pops. Large popsicles shaped like Frankenstein's creature, Dracula, and the Wolfman. Frighteningly delicious embossed on their spines. I wish I could carve these into fun shapes for the boy.

In the room, the old woman puts away her food with ease. She is dipping the banana slices in a non-dairy cream. Poco's food is untouched. The spoon slick with chili abandoned to the side of the bowl.

I can't get him to eat, Anne says, he's barely opened his eyes.

How's his fever, I say.

No better.

Crush some ice. Make a very diluted smoothie for him. Small. Strawberries, blueberries, protein powder, and one of these, I say, slipping her a pill. Crush it and sprinkle it on the top. I think it'll be a couple days before he'll be ready for anything hot.

Anne collects his food and says, I should have known that.

I put my hand on hers. Say, I'm just guessing. The touch feels forced. I know she feels it too.

She smiles, perspiration collecting on the fringe of her lip. It reminds me of dew on spider webs.

Maybe we should put a couple fans in here too.

I take Poco's temperature. Soak a rag in the cool water next to his bed. Wring it partially dry. Wipe his skin. Blow on it. As if he's soup. I'm surprised at how little the old woman says. I barely speak to her. It's as if she's not present. Just a specter jawing at bits of food. Is it guilt? Intimidation? The boy's lips are thin and pale. Nearly chalk. He rouses. His eyes open. Barely. His system so weak. Body so frail. Hey buddy, I say. Then I speak to him in Spanish. Tell him that everything will work out. That he's looking better. He's a vaquero. He'll pull through. I begin to sing to him:

Ven todos, amigos
Para visitar a Mary
Reunámonos alrededor de Tonantzin
Santa María de Guadalupe

His feet move, back and forth. I say things like, that'a'boy, 'lil vaquero. His grandmother asks me how I know the song. How I know how to sing it so well. I tell her I listen to everything around me. To the people. The children. The wind and sea.

Anne returns with the smoothie and Zelda is at her heels. I tell Zelda to sit outside the door. She obeys. The spoon handle is frosty. I wipe the perspiration from my fingers and pull it from the glass. The juice is beginning to absorb the crushed pill, so I pull a spoonful from top and ask Poco to open his mouth. He does. His tongue, a unripe strawberry tucked between his teeth. I slip the spoon into his mouth. Poco closes upon it and sucks it down. Mmm, he says.

¿Ya comiste, zalamero?

No.

I spoon more to him. He eats most of it. Grows tired. Falls to sleep. I carry the dishes away and grab some fans from empty rooms. I fill bowls with ice. Place them in front of the fans. Point them at Poco. His body twitches in his sleep. I open one of the bags and pull from it an oversized bed dress for the old woman. She frowns. Tells me that she can't accept it. It's okay, I tell her, I pay no rent. She doesn't understand me. My Spanish failing. Talking about my money. My lack of need for it. I want to tell her I'm hiding. Avoiding the cut and sizzle of the world up north. That there's nothing to love. Nothing to wake to. That there are suns and moons. That my only desire is to work and sit in the sand. That she can have my money. My years left. My health. And then Poco coughs. He coughs and coughs and his body convulses in fever. I drop the dress on the edge of her bed. Kneel next to Poco. Wipe his forehead clear of sweat. He is crying. The tears hanging on the edges of his eyes. I sit on his bed. Bend over him. His slender arms reach around me. Quédate, he says. His eyes not open. I kiss his forehead. Feel the fever. Mi vaquero, Mi vaquero, ven a casa conmigo, I sing to him in the melody of "In the Pines." My heart, a landslide.

    He falls back into sleep.

    Es hermosa, the old woman says, holding the gown.

    Tú y Arturo se merece cosas buenas, I say.

    Gracias, she says, smiling.

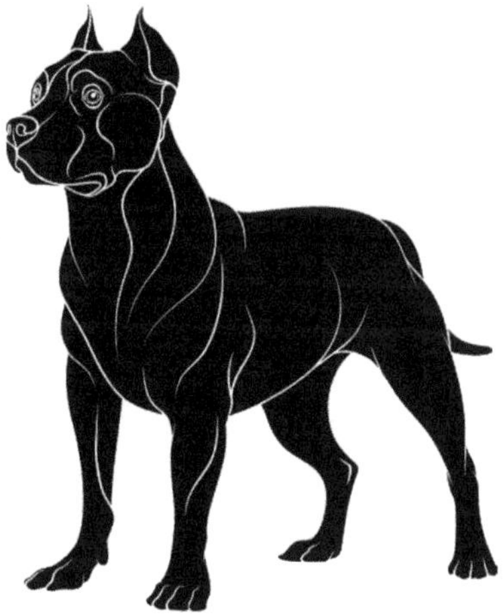

ABOUT DUNCAN B. BARLOW

duncan b. barlow is the author of The City, Awake (Stalking Horse 2017), Of Flesh and Fur (The Cupboard 2016), and Super Cell Anemia (2008). He teaches creative writing at the University of South Dakota, where he is publisher at Astrophil Press and the managing editor at South Dakota Review. He lives in South Dakota with his cat, Monkey.

www.duncanbbarlow.com

CPSIA information can be obtained
at www.ICGtesting.com
Printed in the USA
FFHW020735130619
52969481-58586FF